MUMMY

Adapted by
Bart A. Thompson

Illustrated by
Brian Miroglio

Based upon the works of
Bram Stoker

magic
wagon

visit us at
www.abdopublishing.com

Published by Magic Wagon, a division of the ABDO Publishing Group, 8000 West 78th Street, Edina, Minnesota 55439. Copyright © 2008 by Abdo Consulting Group, Inc. International copyrights reserved in all countries. All rights reserved. No part of this book may be reproduced in any form without written permission from the publisher. Graphic Planet™ is a trademark and logo of Magic Wagon.

Printed in the United States.

Based upon the works of Bram Stoker
Written by Bart A. Thompson
Illustrated by Brian Miroglio
Letters and colors by Lynx Studio
Edited & Directed by Chazz DeMoss
Cover Design by Neil Klinepier

Library of Congress Cataloging-in-Publication Data

Thompson, Bart A.
  Mummy / written by Bart A. Thompson ; based upon the works of Bram Stoker.
      p. cm.
  ISBN-13: 978-1-60270-061-1
  1. Graphic novels. I. Stoker, Bram, 1847-1912. II. Title.
  PN6727.T32M86 2008
  741.5'973--dc22

                                        2007016370

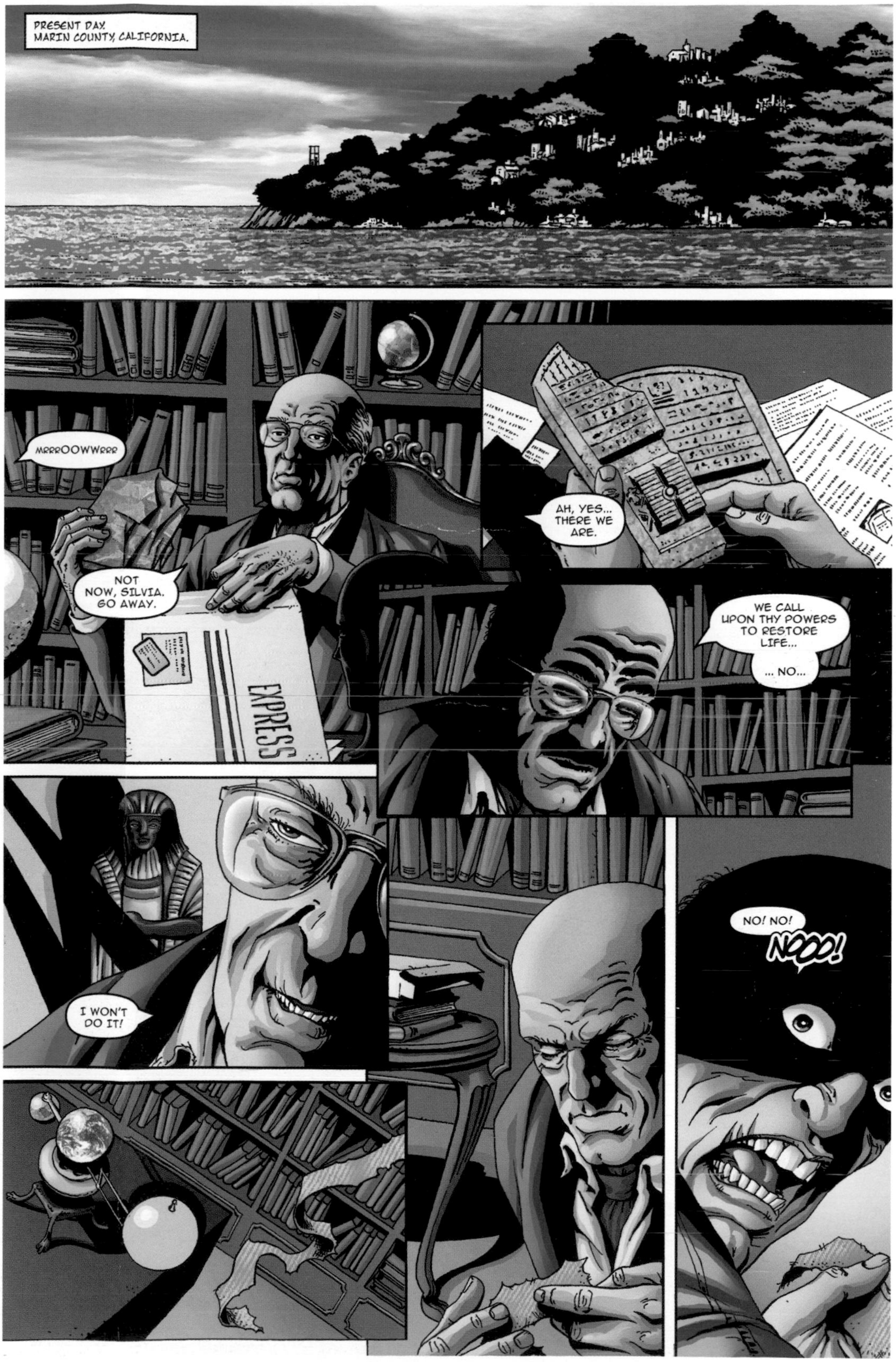
PRESENT DAY.
MARIN COUNTY, CALIFORNIA.
MRRROOWWRRR
NOT NOW, SILVIA. GO AWAY.
EXPRESS
AH, YES... THERE WE ARE.
WE CALL UPON THY POWERS TO RESTORE LIFE...
... NO...
I WON'T DO IT!
NO! NO!
NOOO!

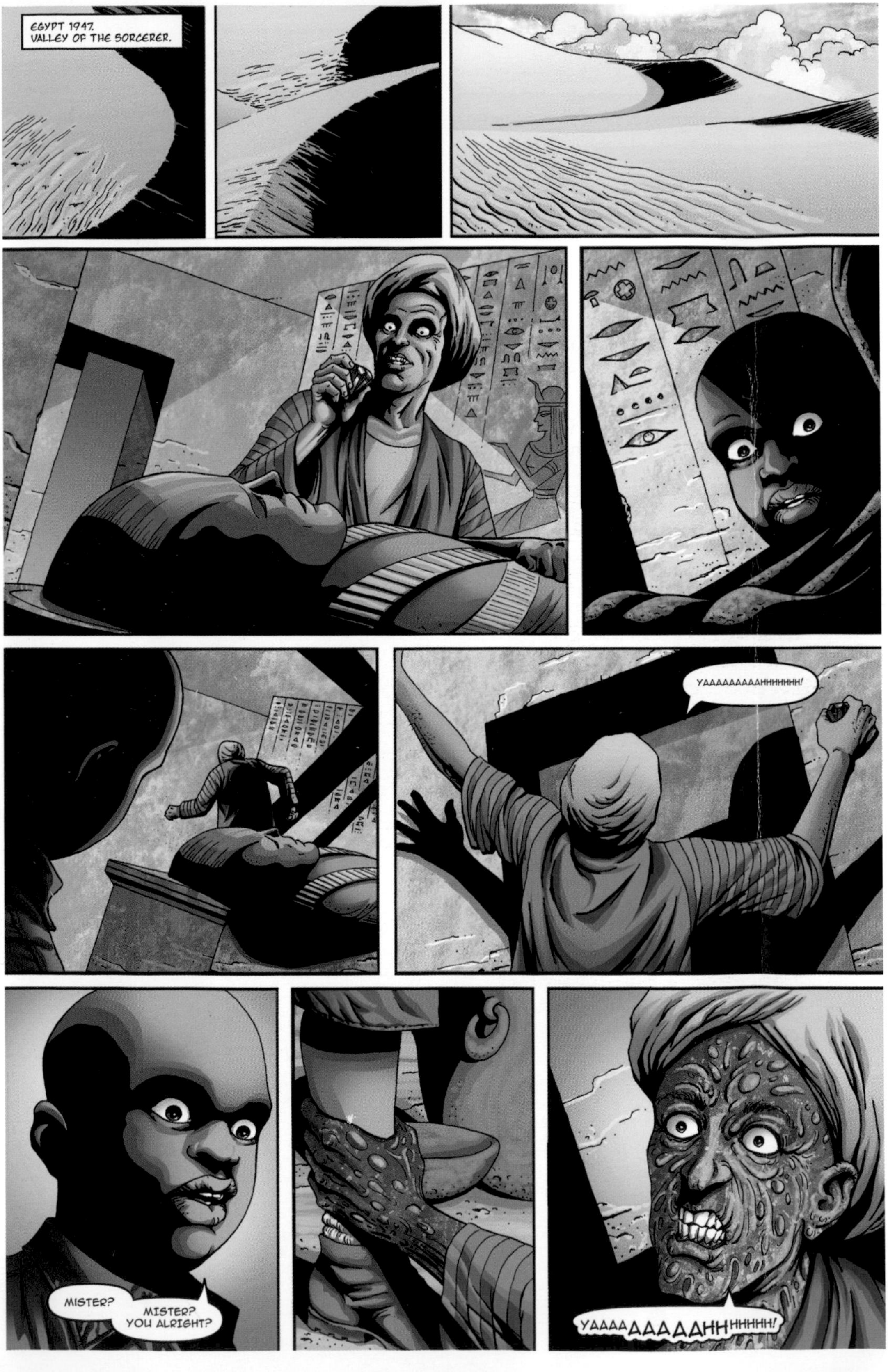
EGYPT 1947.
VALLEY OF THE SORCERER.
YAAAAAAAAAAHHHHHHH!
MISTER?
MISTER? YOU ALRIGHT?
YAAAAAAAAAHHHHHHH!

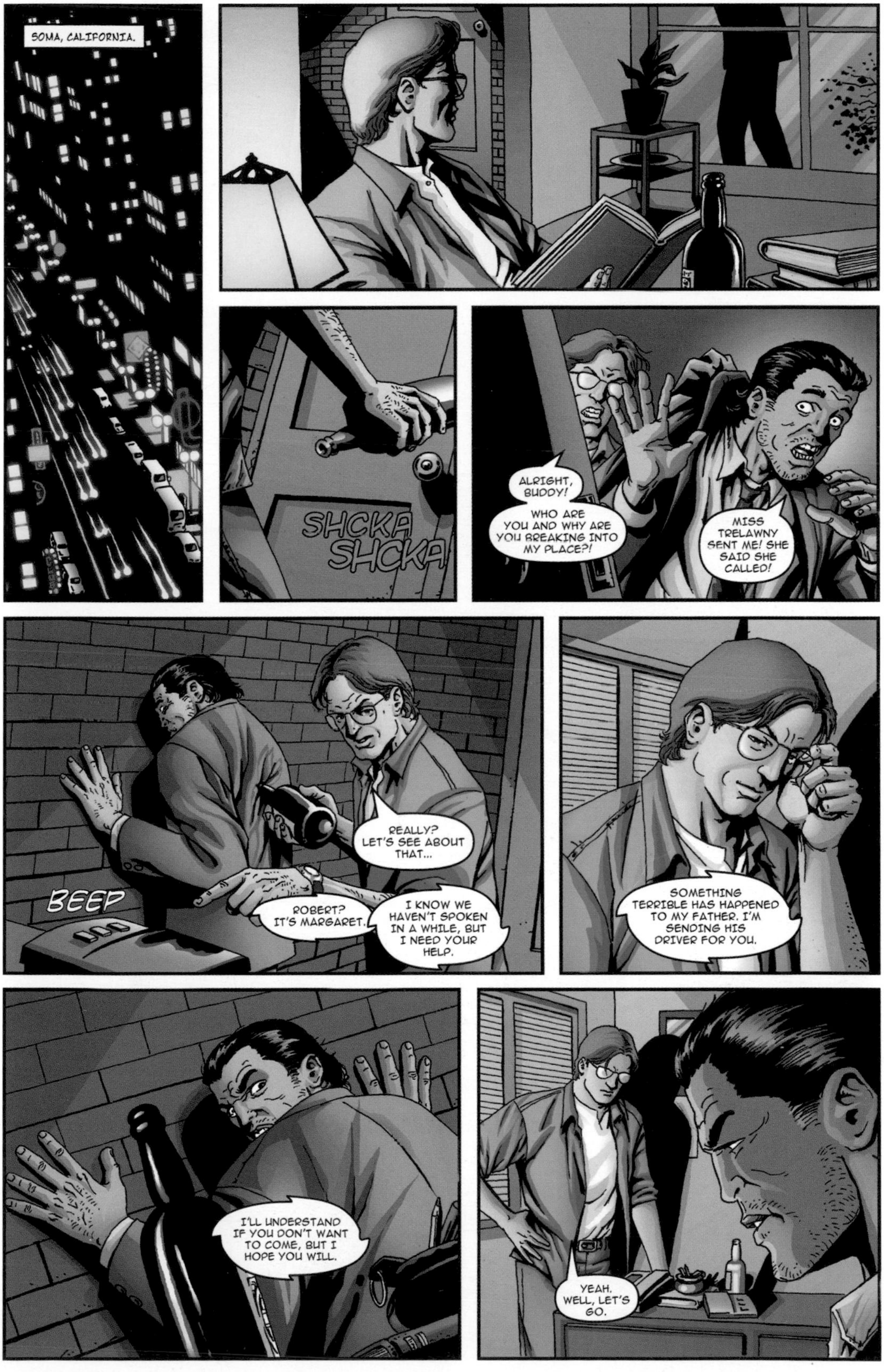
SOMA, CALIFORNIA.
SHCKA SHCKA
ALRIGHT, BUDDY!
WHO ARE YOU AND WHY ARE YOU BREAKING INTO MY PLACE?!
MISS TRELAWNY SENT ME! SHE SAID SHE CALLED!
REALLY? LET'S SEE ABOUT THAT...
BEEP
ROBERT? IT'S MARGARET.
I KNOW WE HAVEN'T SPOKEN IN A WHILE, BUT I NEED YOUR HELP.
SOMETHING TERRIBLE HAS HAPPENED TO MY FATHER. I'M SENDING HIS DRIVER FOR YOU.
I'LL UNDERSTAND IF YOU DON'T WANT TO COME, BUT I HOPE YOU WILL.
YEAH. WELL, LET'S GO.

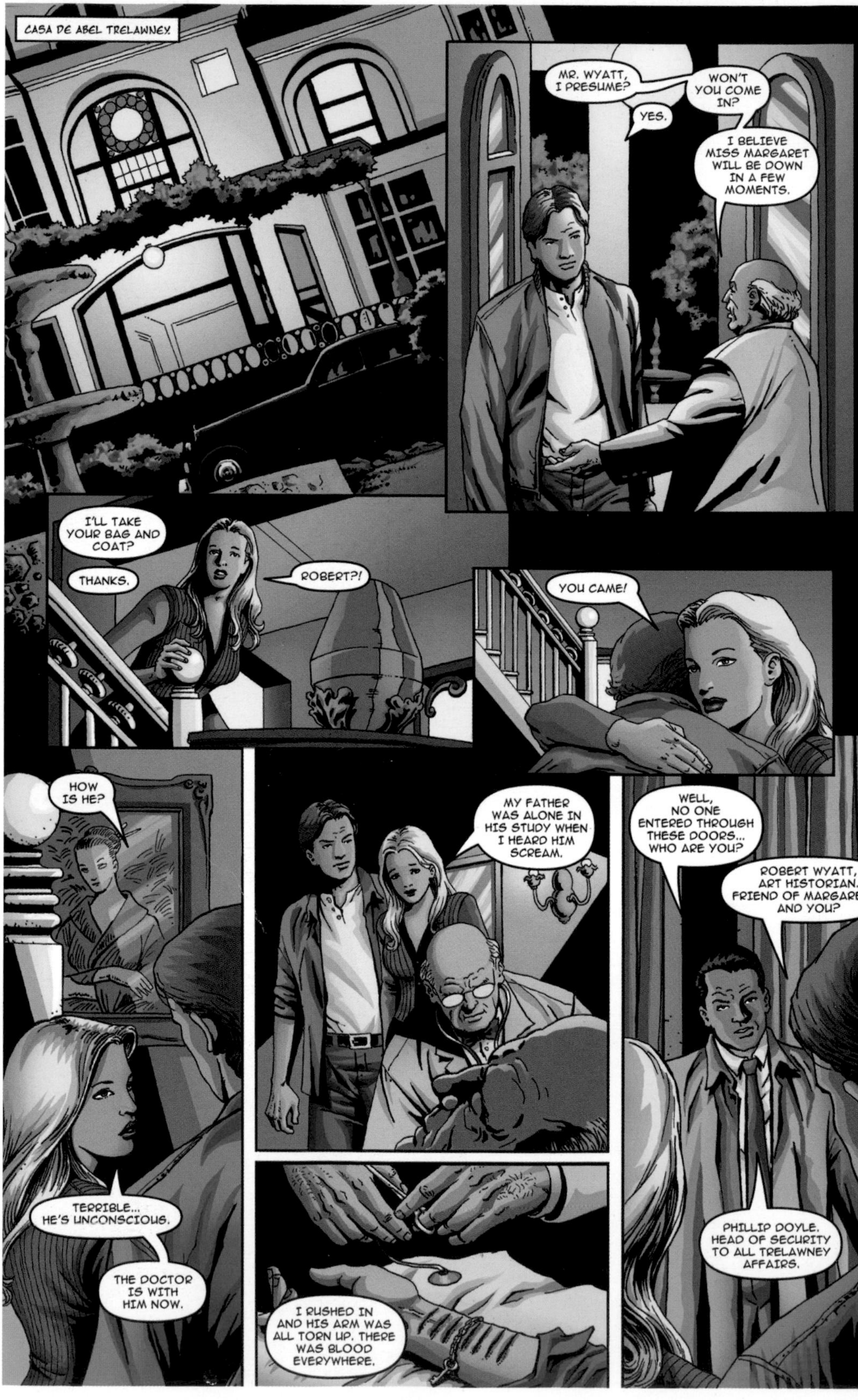

CASA DE ABEL TRELAWNEY.
MR. WYATT, I PRESUME?
YES.
WON'T YOU COME IN?
I BELIEVE MISS MARGARET WILL BE DOWN IN A FEW MOMENTS.
I'LL TAKE YOUR BAG AND COAT?
THANKS.
ROBERT?!
YOU CAME!
HOW IS HE?
TERRIBLE... HE'S UNCONSCIOUS.
THE DOCTOR IS WITH HIM NOW.
MY FATHER WAS ALONE IN HIS STUDY WHEN I HEARD HIM SCREAM.
I RUSHED IN AND HIS ARM WAS ALL TORN UP. THERE WAS BLOOD EVERYWHERE.
WELL, NO ONE ENTERED THROUGH THESE DOORS... WHO ARE YOU?
ROBERT WYATT, ART HISTORIAN. FRIEND OF MARGARET'S. AND YOU?
PHILLIP DOYLE. HEAD OF SECURITY TO ALL TRELAWNEY AFFAIRS.

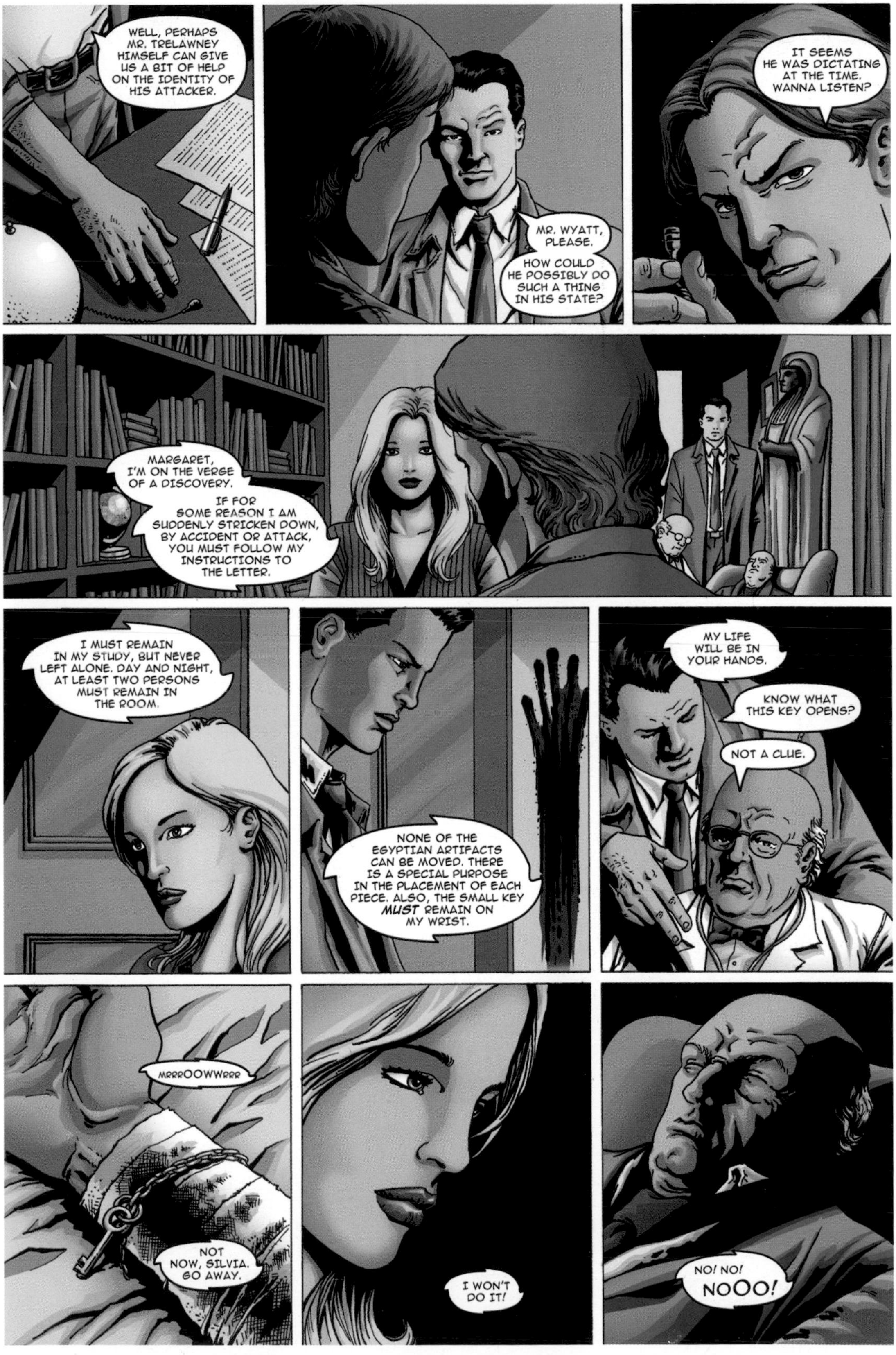

WELL, PERHAPS MR. TRELAWNEY HIMSELF CAN GIVE US A BIT OF HELP ON THE IDENTITY OF HIS ATTACKER.
MR. WYATT, PLEASE.
HOW COULD HE POSSIBLY DO SUCH A THING IN HIS STATE?
IT SEEMS HE WAS DICTATING AT THE TIME. WANNA LISTEN?
MARGARET, I'M ON THE VERGE OF A DISCOVERY.
IF FOR SOME REASON I AM SUDDENLY STRICKEN DOWN, BY ACCIDENT OR ATTACK, YOU MUST FOLLOW MY INSTRUCTIONS TO THE LETTER.
I MUST REMAIN IN MY STUDY, BUT NEVER LEFT ALONE. DAY AND NIGHT, AT LEAST TWO PERSONS MUST REMAIN IN THE ROOM.
NONE OF THE EGYPTIAN ARTIFACTS CAN BE MOVED. THERE IS A SPECIAL PURPOSE IN THE PLACEMENT OF EACH PIECE. ALSO, THE SMALL KEY *MUST* REMAIN ON MY WRIST.
MY LIFE WILL BE IN YOUR HANDS.
KNOW WHAT THIS KEY OPENS?
NOT A CLUE.
mrrrOOWWrrr
NOT NOW, SILVIA. GO AWAY.
I WON'T DO IT!
NO! NO! NOOO!

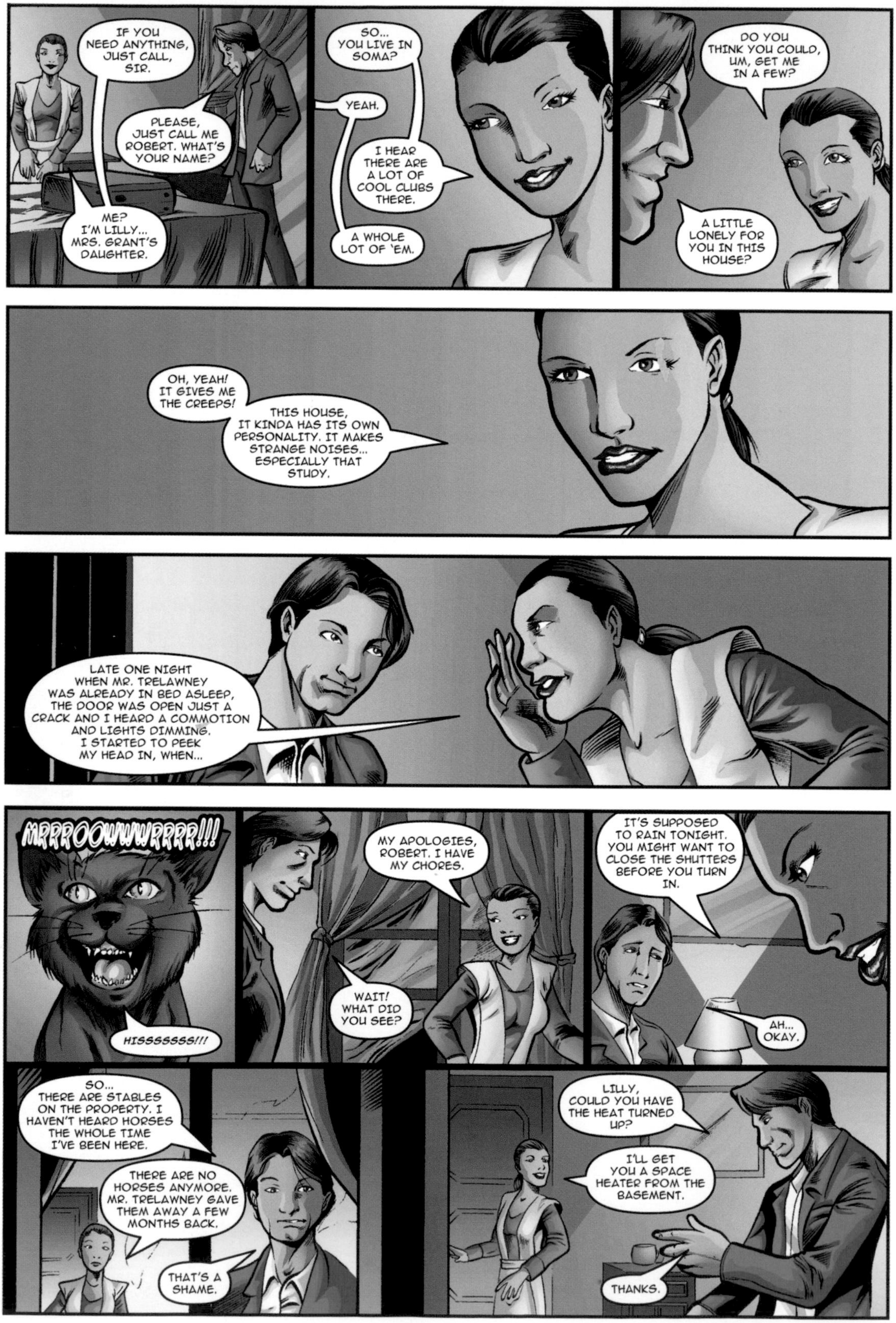
IF YOU NEED ANYTHING, JUST CALL, SIR.
PLEASE, JUST CALL ME ROBERT. WHAT'S YOUR NAME?
ME? I'M LILLY... MRS. GRANT'S DAUGHTER.
SO... YOU LIVE IN SOMA?
YEAH.
I HEAR THERE ARE A LOT OF COOL CLUBS THERE.
A WHOLE LOT OF 'EM.
DO YOU THINK YOU COULD, UM, GET ME IN A FEW?
A LITTLE LONELY FOR YOU IN THIS HOUSE?
OH, YEAH! IT GIVES ME THE CREEPS!
THIS HOUSE, IT KINDA HAS ITS OWN PERSONALITY. IT MAKES STRANGE NOISES... ESPECIALLY THAT STUDY.
LATE ONE NIGHT WHEN MR. TRELAWNEY WAS ALREADY IN BED ASLEEP, THE DOOR WAS OPEN JUST A CRACK AND I HEARD A COMMOTION AND LIGHTS DIMMING. I STARTED TO PEEK MY HEAD IN, WHEN...
MRRROOWWWRRRR!!!
HISSSSSSS!!!
MY APOLOGIES, ROBERT. I HAVE MY CHORES.
WAIT! WHAT DID YOU SEE?
IT'S SUPPOSED TO RAIN TONIGHT. YOU MIGHT WANT TO CLOSE THE SHUTTERS BEFORE YOU TURN IN.
AH... OKAY.
SO... THERE ARE STABLES ON THE PROPERTY. I HAVEN'T HEARD HORSES THE WHOLE TIME I'VE BEEN HERE.
THERE ARE NO HORSES ANYMORE. MR. TRELAWNEY GAVE THEM AWAY A FEW MONTHS BACK.
THAT'S A SHAME.
LILLY, COULD YOU HAVE THE HEAT TURNED UP?
I'LL GET YOU A SPACE HEATER FROM THE BASEMENT.
THANKS.

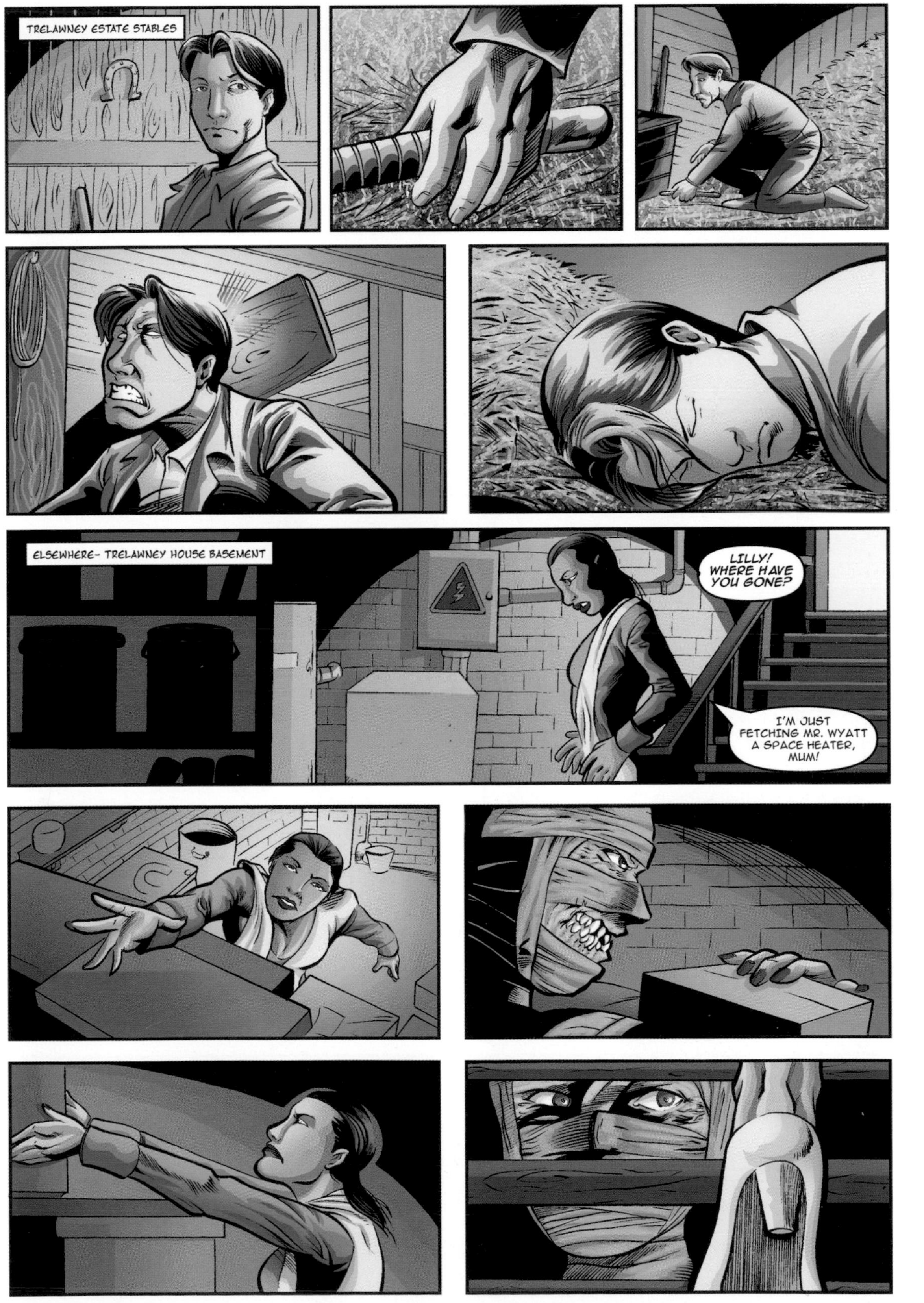
TRELAWNEY ESTATE STABLES
ELSEWHERE- TRELAWNEY HOUSE BASEMENT
LILLY! WHERE HAVE YOU GONE?
I'M JUST FETCHING MR. WYATT A SPACE HEATER, MUM!

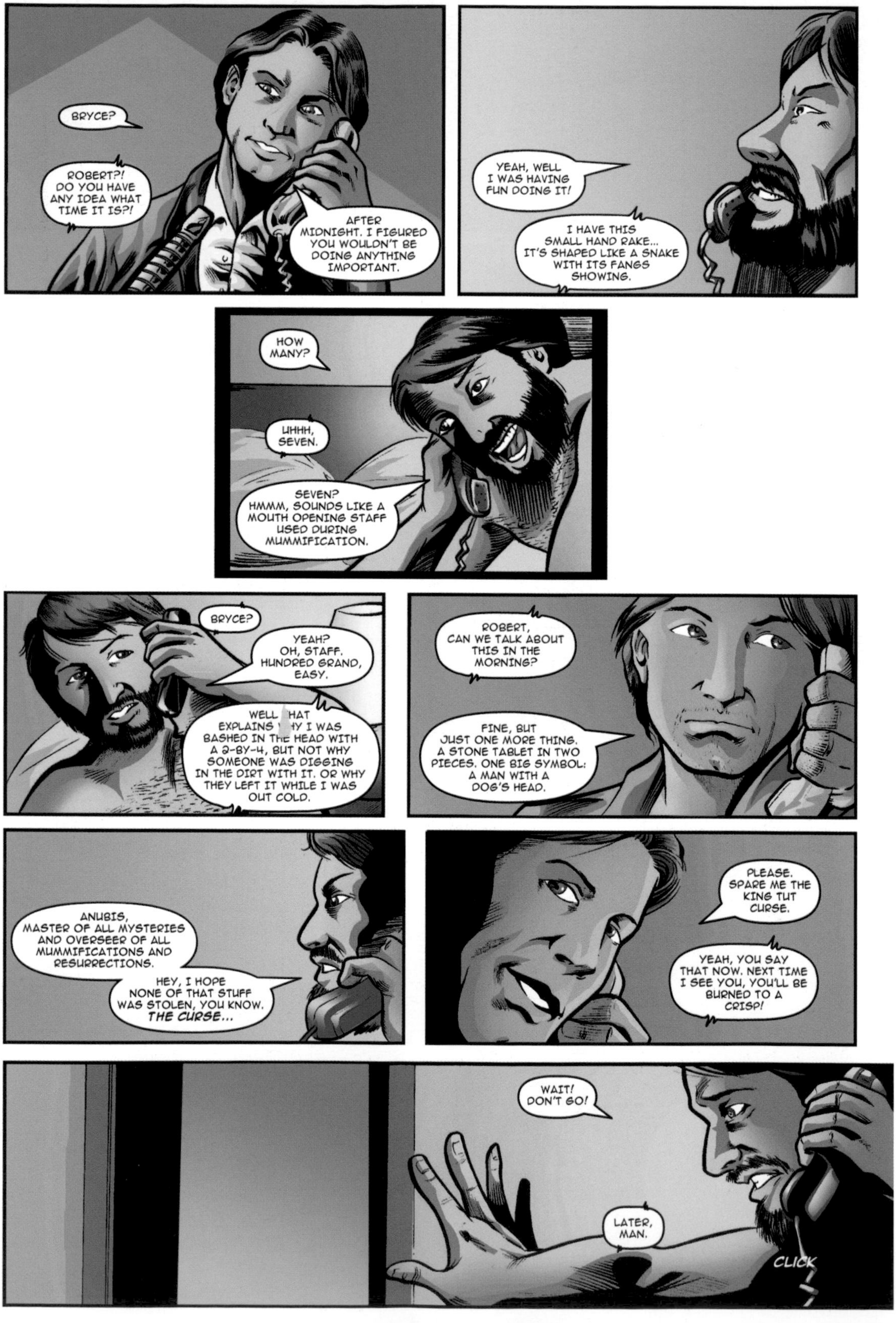
BRYCE?
ROBERT?! DO YOU HAVE ANY IDEA WHAT TIME IT IS?!
AFTER MIDNIGHT. I FIGURED YOU WOULDN'T BE DOING ANYTHING IMPORTANT.
YEAH, WELL I WAS HAVING FUN DOING IT!
I HAVE THIS SMALL HAND RAKE... IT'S SHAPED LIKE A SNAKE WITH ITS FANGS SHOWING.
HOW MANY?
UHHH, SEVEN.
SEVEN? HMMM, SOUNDS LIKE A MOUTH OPENING STAFF USED DURING MUMMIFICATION.
BRYCE?
YEAH? OH, STAFF. HUNDRED GRAND, EASY.
WELL THAT EXPLAINS WHY I WAS BASHED IN THE HEAD WITH A 2-BY-4, BUT NOT WHY SOMEONE WAS DIGGING IN THE DIRT WITH IT. OR WHY THEY LEFT IT WHILE I WAS OUT COLD.
ROBERT, CAN WE TALK ABOUT THIS IN THE MORNING?
FINE, BUT JUST ONE MORE THING. A STONE TABLET IN TWO PIECES. ONE BIG SYMBOL: A MAN WITH A DOG'S HEAD.
ANUBIS, MASTER OF ALL MYSTERIES AND OVERSEER OF ALL MUMMIFICATIONS AND RESURRECTIONS.
HEY, I HOPE NONE OF THAT STUFF WAS STOLEN, YOU KNOW. *THE CURSE...*
PLEASE. SPARE ME THE KING TUT CURSE.
YEAH, YOU SAY THAT NOW. NEXT TIME I SEE YOU, YOU'LL BE BURNED TO A CRISP!
WAIT! DON'T GO!
LATER, MAN.
CLICK

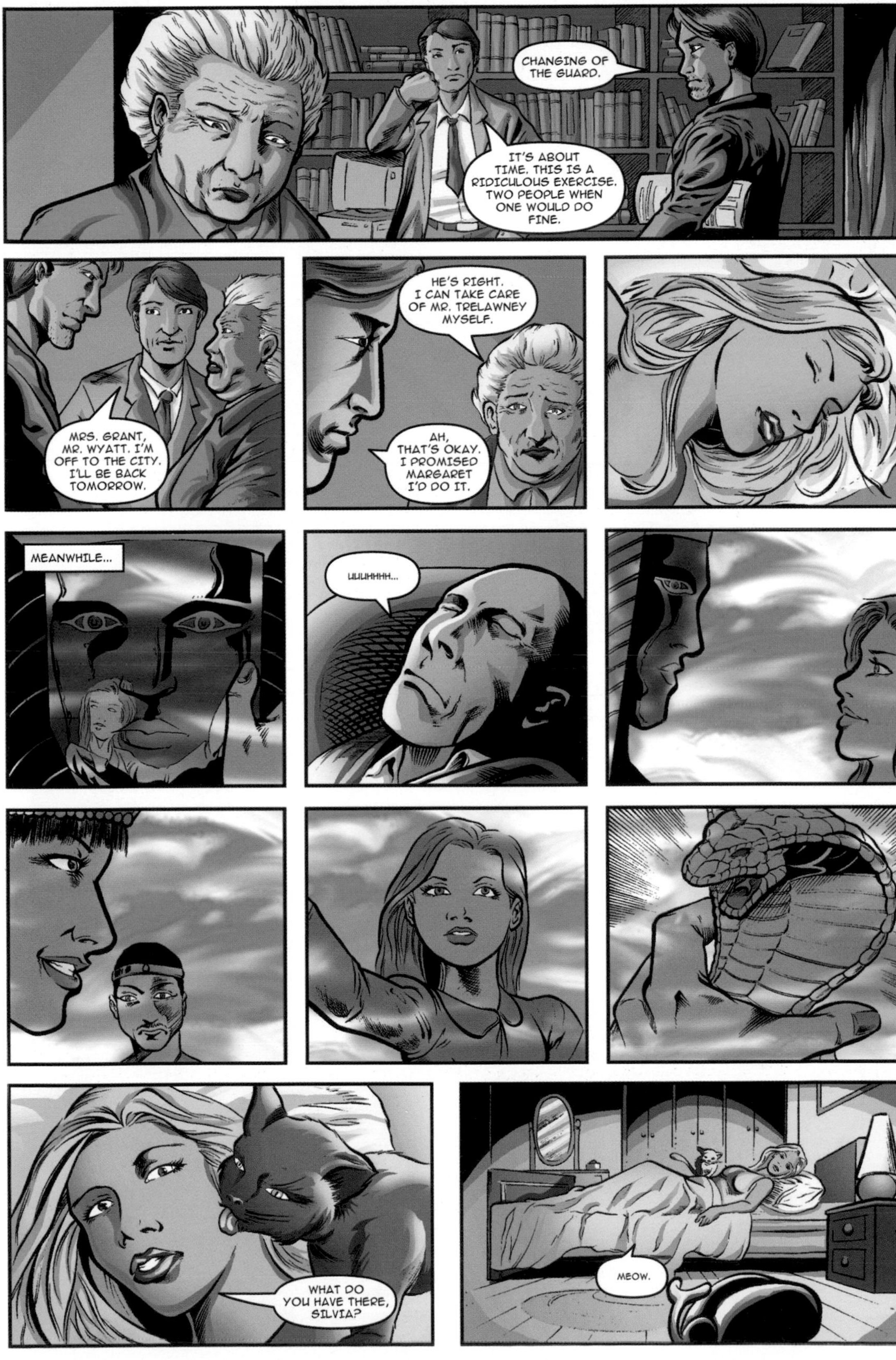
CHANGING OF THE GUARD.
IT'S ABOUT TIME. THIS IS A RIDICULOUS EXERCISE. TWO PEOPLE WHEN ONE WOULD DO FINE.
MRS. GRANT, MR. WYATT. I'M OFF TO THE CITY. I'LL BE BACK TOMORROW.
HE'S RIGHT. I CAN TAKE CARE OF MR. TRELAWNEY MYSELF.
AH, THAT'S OKAY. I PROMISED MARGARET I'D DO IT.
MEANWHILE...
UUUHHHH...
WHAT DO YOU HAVE THERE, SILVIA?
MEOW.

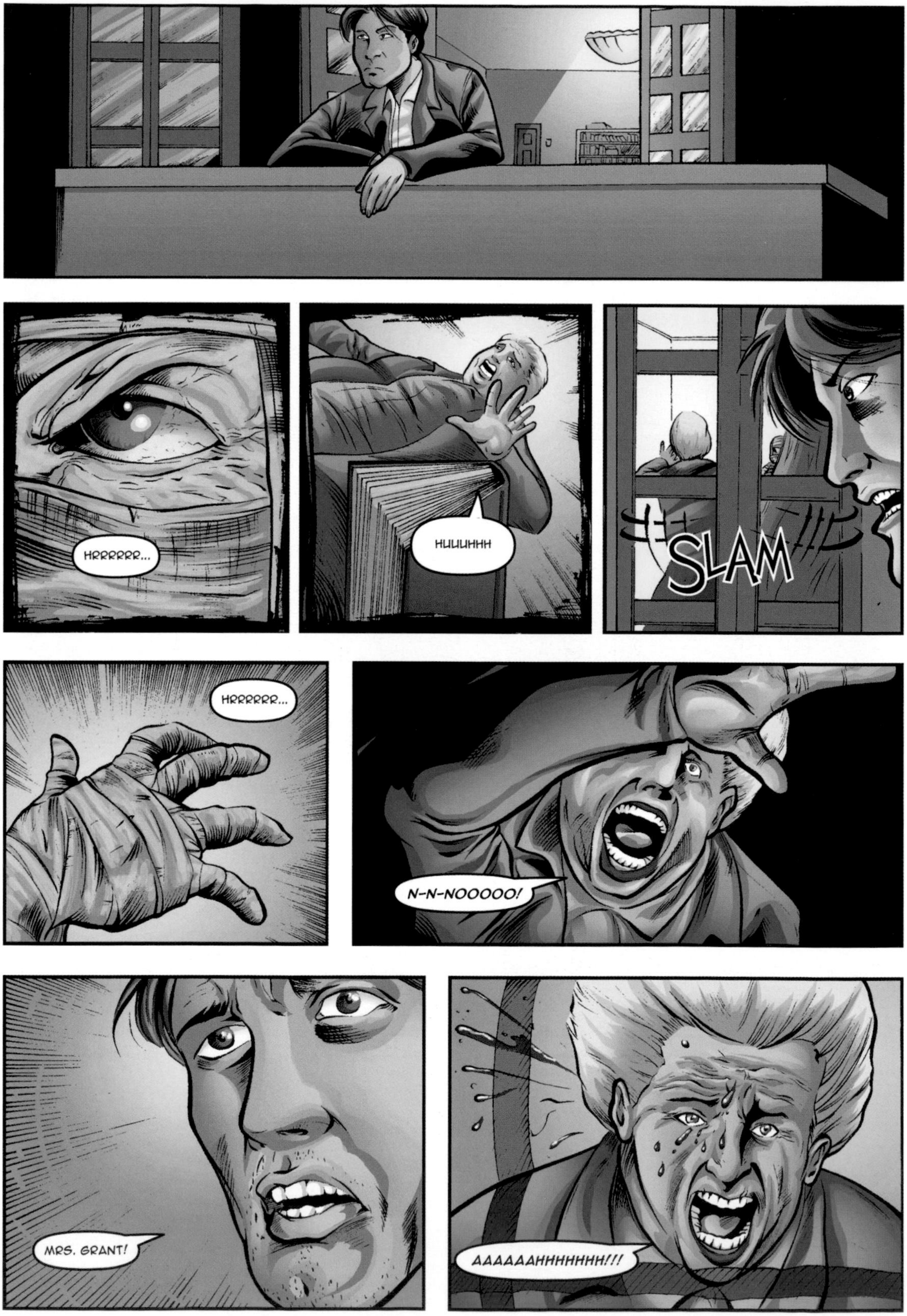
HRRRRRR...
HUUUHHH
SLAM
HRRRRRR...
N-N-NOOOOO!
MRS. GRANT!
AAAAAAHHHHHHH!!!

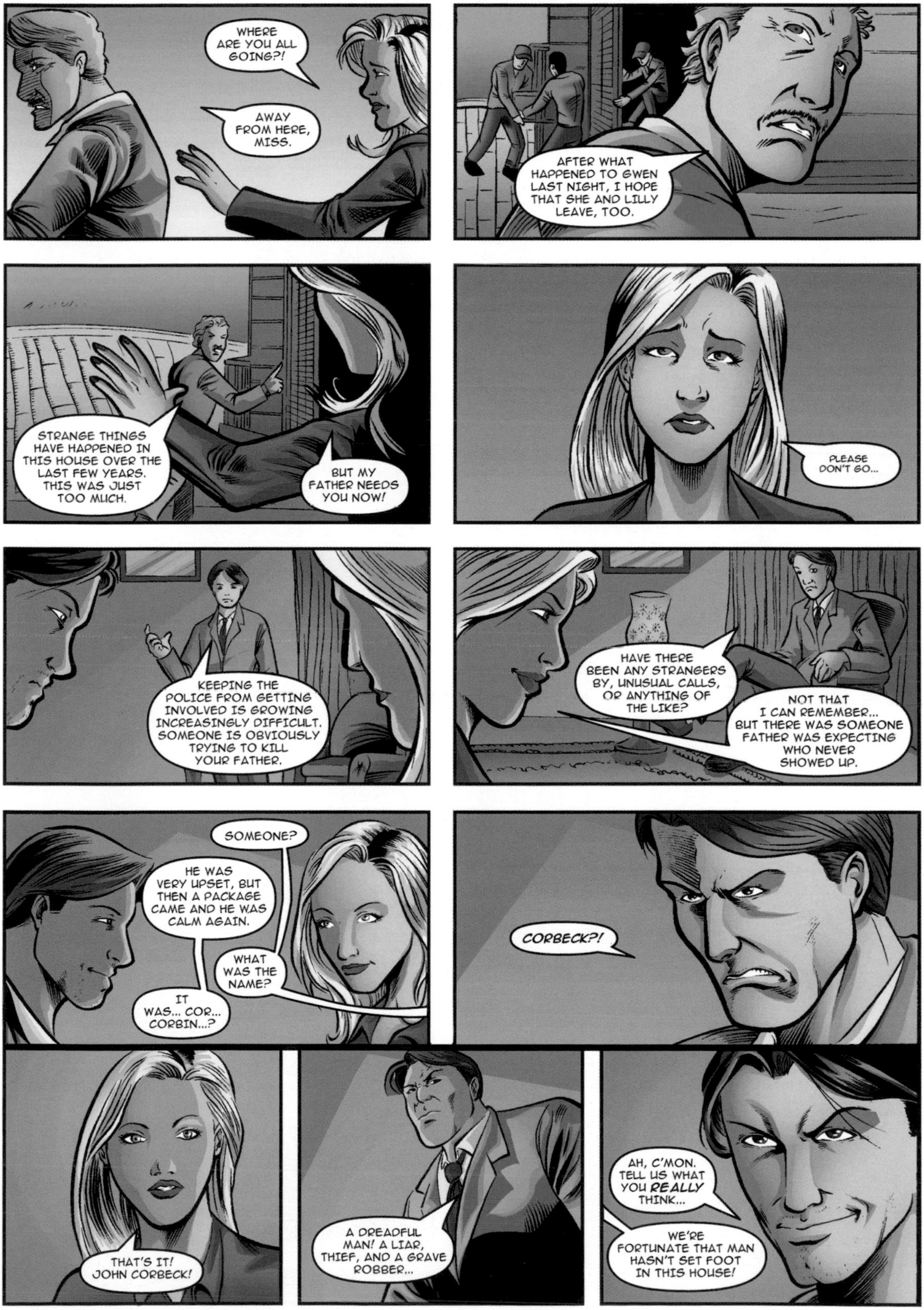
WHERE ARE YOU ALL GOING?!
AWAY FROM HERE, MISS.
AFTER WHAT HAPPENED TO GWEN LAST NIGHT, I HOPE THAT SHE AND LILLY LEAVE, TOO.
STRANGE THINGS HAVE HAPPENED IN THIS HOUSE OVER THE LAST FEW YEARS. THIS WAS JUST TOO MUCH.
BUT MY FATHER NEEDS YOU NOW!
PLEASE DON'T GO...
KEEPING THE POLICE FROM GETTING INVOLVED IS GROWING INCREASINGLY DIFFICULT. SOMEONE IS OBVIOUSLY TRYING TO KILL YOUR FATHER.
HAVE THERE BEEN ANY STRANGERS BY, UNUSUAL CALLS, OR ANYTHING OF THE LIKE?
NOT THAT I CAN REMEMBER... BUT THERE WAS SOMEONE FATHER WAS EXPECTING WHO NEVER SHOWED UP.
SOMEONE?
HE WAS VERY UPSET, BUT THEN A PACKAGE CAME AND HE WAS CALM AGAIN.
WHAT WAS THE NAME?
IT WAS... COR... CORBIN...?
CORBECK?!
THAT'S IT! JOHN CORBECK!
A DREADFUL MAN! A LIAR, THIEF, AND A GRAVE ROBBER...
AH, C'MON. TELL US WHAT YOU REALLY THINK...
WE'RE FORTUNATE THAT MAN HASN'T SET FOOT IN THIS HOUSE!

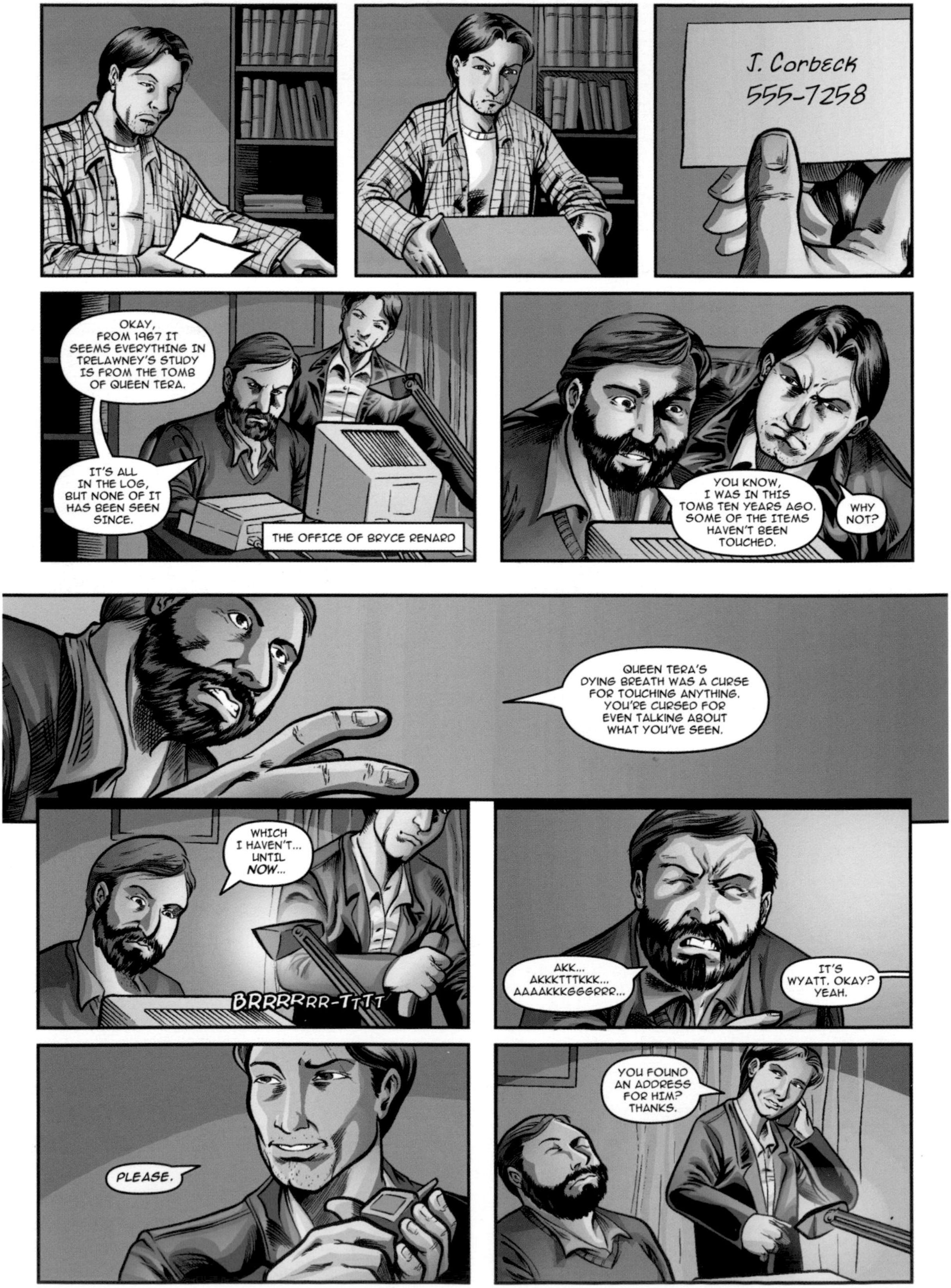
J. Corbeck
555-7258
OKAY, FROM 1967 IT SEEMS EVERYTHING IN TRELAWNEY'S STUDY IS FROM THE TOMB OF QUEEN TERA.
IT'S ALL IN THE LOG, BUT NONE OF IT HAS BEEN SEEN SINCE.
THE OFFICE OF BRYCE RENARD
YOU KNOW, I WAS IN THIS TOMB TEN YEARS AGO. SOME OF THE ITEMS HAVEN'T BEEN TOUCHED.
WHY NOT?
QUEEN TERA'S DYING BREATH WAS A CURSE FOR TOUCHING ANYTHING. YOU'RE CURSED FOR EVEN TALKING ABOUT WHAT YOU'VE SEEN.
WHICH I HAVEN'T... UNTIL NOW...
BRRRRRR-TTTT
AKK... AKKKTTTKKK... AAAAKKKGGGRRR...
IT'S WYATT. OKAY? YEAH.
PLEASE.
YOU FOUND AN ADDRESS FOR HIM? THANKS.

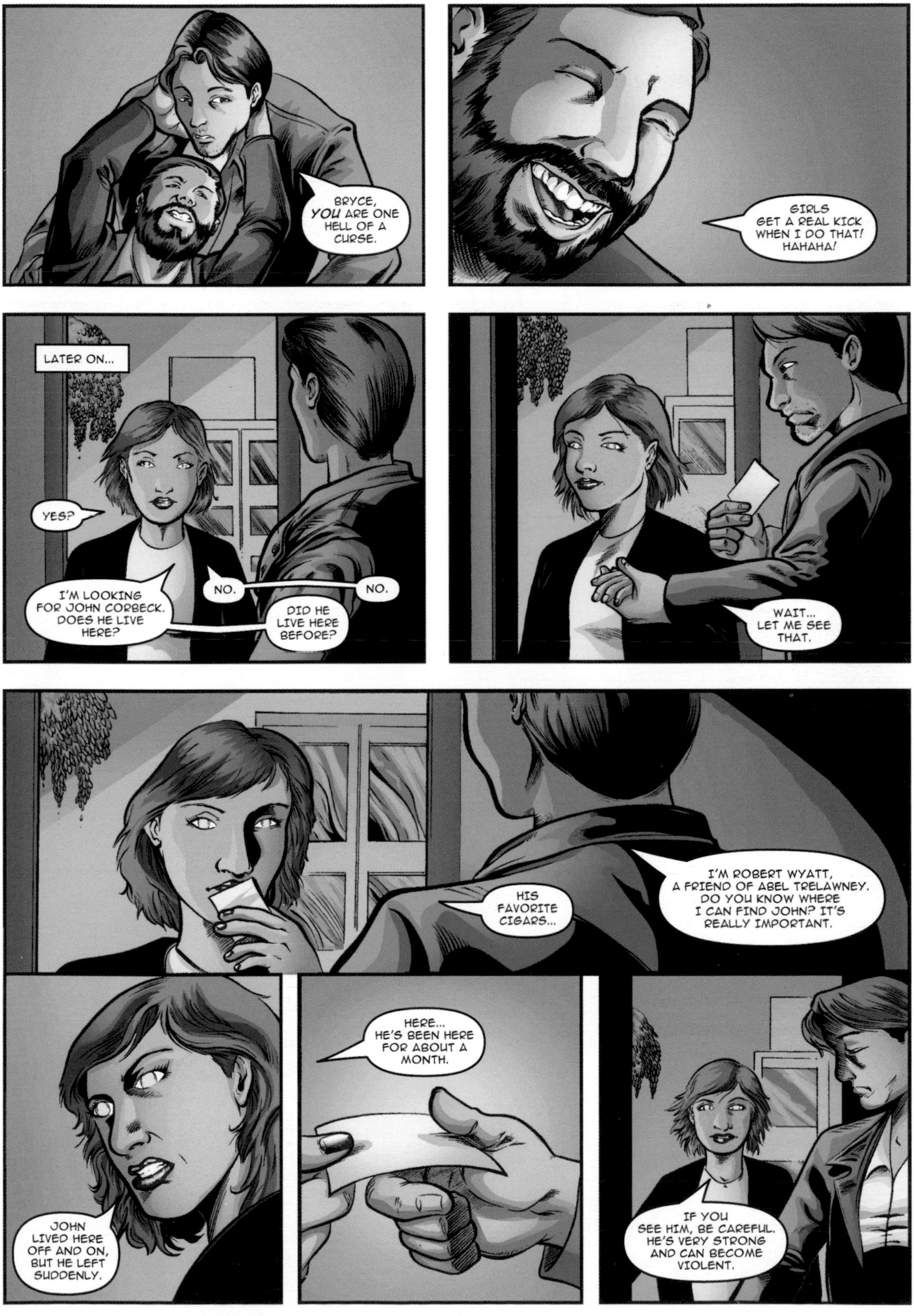
BRYCE, YOU ARE ONE HELL OF A CURSE.
GIRLS GET A REAL KICK WHEN I DO THAT! HAHAHA!
LATER ON...
YES?
I'M LOOKING FOR JOHN CORBECK. DOES HE LIVE HERE?
NO.
DID HE LIVE HERE BEFORE?
NO.
WAIT... LET ME SEE THAT.
HIS FAVORITE CIGARS...
I'M ROBERT WYATT, A FRIEND OF ABEL TRELAWNEY. DO YOU KNOW WHERE I CAN FIND JOHN? IT'S REALLY IMPORTANT.
JOHN LIVED HERE OFF AND ON, BUT HE LEFT SUDDENLY.
HERE... HE'S BEEN HERE FOR ABOUT A MONTH.
IF YOU SEE HIM, BE CAREFUL. HE'S VERY STRONG AND CAN BECOME VIOLENT.

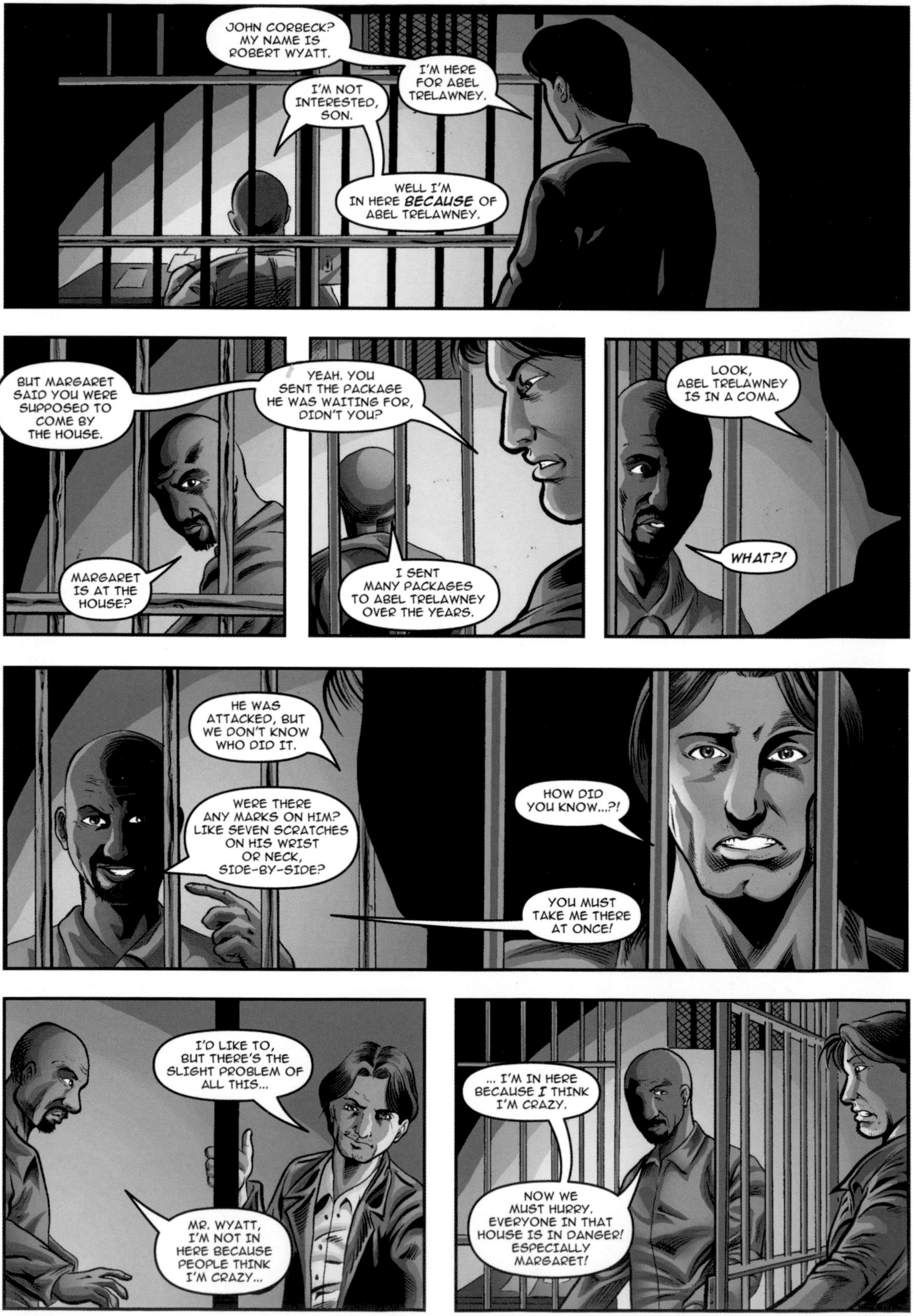
JOHN CORBECK? MY NAME IS ROBERT WYATT.
I'M HERE FOR ABEL TRELAWNEY.
I'M NOT INTERESTED, SON.
WELL I'M IN HERE *BECAUSE* OF ABEL TRELAWNEY.
BUT MARGARET SAID YOU WERE SUPPOSED TO COME BY THE HOUSE.
MARGARET IS AT THE HOUSE?
YEAH. YOU SENT THE PACKAGE HE WAS WAITING FOR, DIDN'T YOU?
I SENT MANY PACKAGES TO ABEL TRELAWNEY OVER THE YEARS.
LOOK, ABEL TRELAWNEY IS IN A COMA.
WHAT?!
HE WAS ATTACKED, BUT WE DON'T KNOW WHO DID IT.
WERE THERE ANY MARKS ON HIM? LIKE SEVEN SCRATCHES ON HIS WRIST OR NECK, SIDE-BY-SIDE?
HOW DID YOU KNOW...?!
YOU MUST TAKE ME THERE AT ONCE!
I'D LIKE TO, BUT THERE'S THE SLIGHT PROBLEM OF ALL THIS...
MR. WYATT, I'M NOT IN HERE BECAUSE PEOPLE THINK I'M CRAZY...
... I'M IN HERE BECAUSE *I* THINK I'M CRAZY.
NOW WE MUST HURRY. EVERYONE IN THAT HOUSE IS IN DANGER! ESPECIALLY MARGARET!

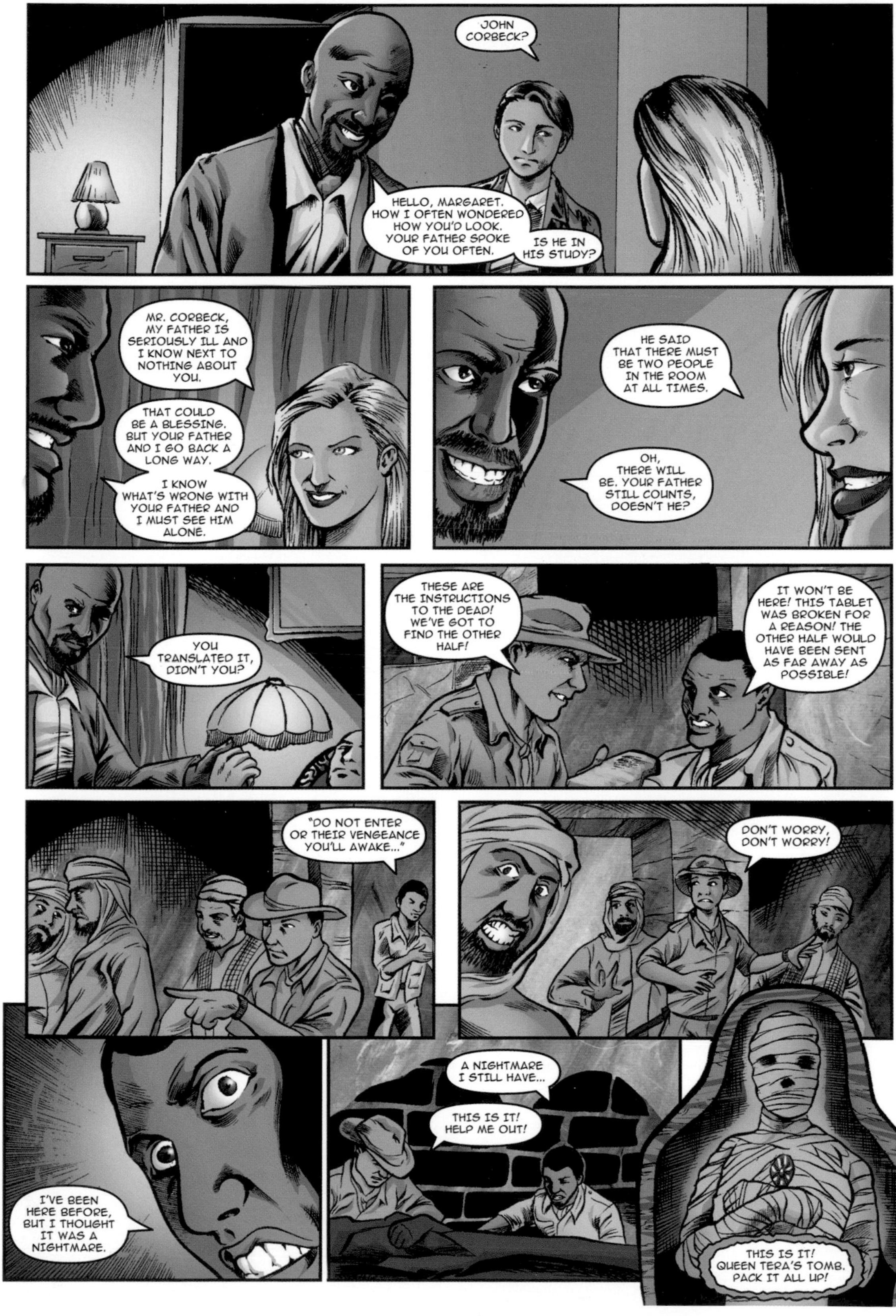
JOHN CORBECK?
HELLO, MARGARET. HOW I OFTEN WONDERED HOW YOU'D LOOK. YOUR FATHER SPOKE OF YOU OFTEN.
IS HE IN HIS STUDY?
MR. CORBECK, MY FATHER IS SERIOUSLY ILL AND I KNOW NEXT TO NOTHING ABOUT YOU.
THAT COULD BE A BLESSING. BUT YOUR FATHER AND I GO BACK A LONG WAY.
I KNOW WHAT'S WRONG WITH YOUR FATHER AND I MUST SEE HIM ALONE.
HE SAID THAT THERE MUST BE TWO PEOPLE IN THE ROOM AT ALL TIMES.
OH, THERE WILL BE. YOUR FATHER STILL COUNTS, DOESN'T HE?
YOU TRANSLATED IT, DIDN'T YOU?
THESE ARE THE INSTRUCTIONS TO THE DEAD! WE'VE GOT TO FIND THE OTHER HALF!
IT WON'T BE HERE! THIS TABLET WAS BROKEN FOR A REASON! THE OTHER HALF WOULD HAVE BEEN SENT AS FAR AWAY AS POSSIBLE!
"DO NOT ENTER OR THEIR VENGEANCE YOU'LL AWAKE..."
DON'T WORRY, DON'T WORRY!
I'VE BEEN HERE BEFORE, BUT I THOUGHT IT WAS A NIGHTMARE.
A NIGHTMARE I STILL HAVE...
THIS IS IT! HELP ME OUT!
THIS IS IT! QUEEN TERA'S TOMB. PACK IT ALL UP!

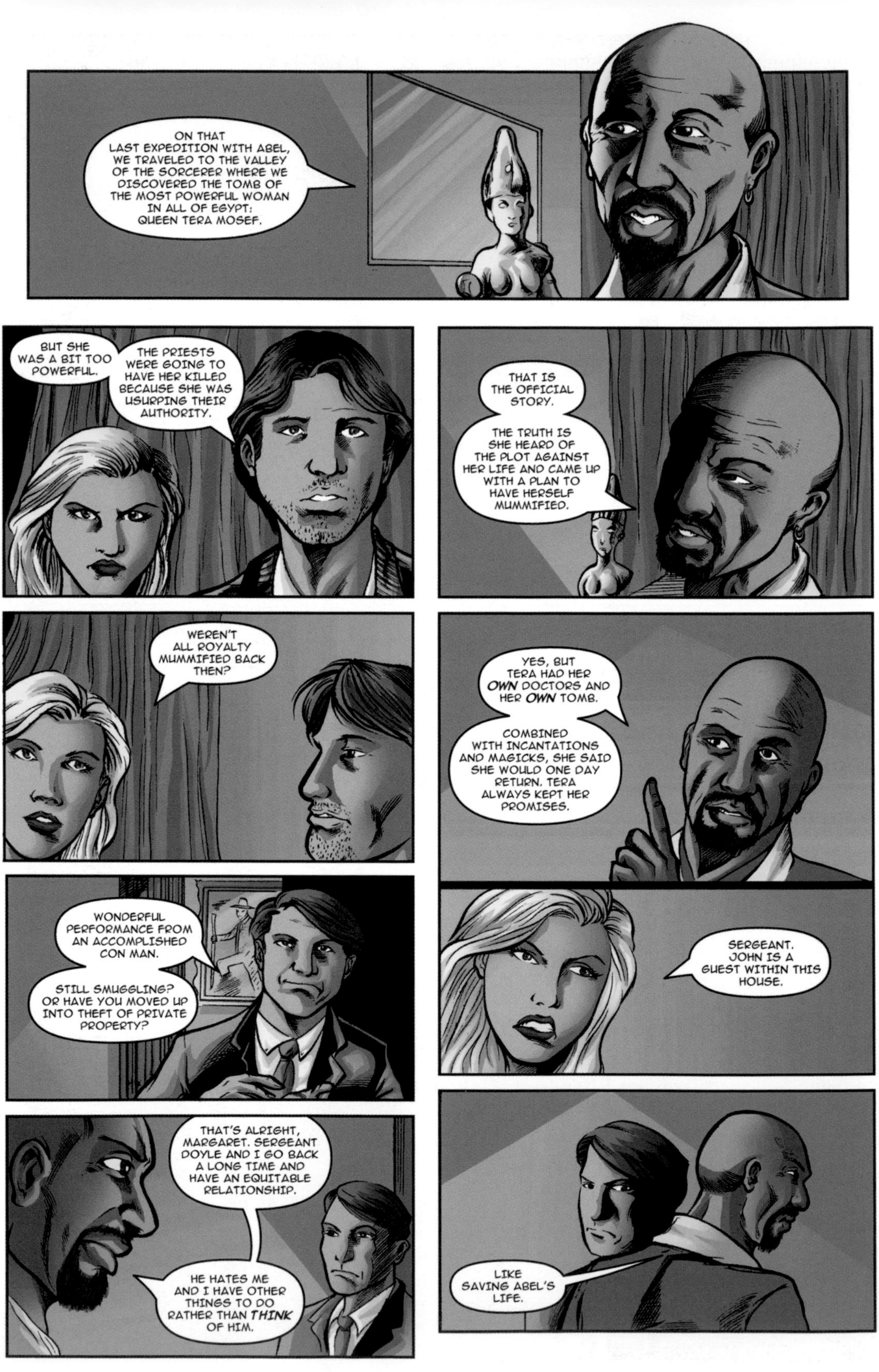
ON THAT LAST EXPEDITION WITH ABEL, WE TRAVELED TO THE VALLEY OF THE SORCERER WHERE WE DISCOVERED THE TOMB OF THE MOST POWERFUL WOMAN IN ALL OF EGYPT: QUEEN TERA MOSEF.
BUT SHE WAS A BIT TOO POWERFUL.
THE PRIESTS WERE GOING TO HAVE HER KILLED BECAUSE SHE WAS USURPING THEIR AUTHORITY.
THAT IS THE OFFICIAL STORY.
THE TRUTH IS SHE HEARD OF THE PLOT AGAINST HER LIFE AND CAME UP WITH A PLAN TO HAVE HERSELF MUMMIFIED.
WEREN'T ALL ROYALTY MUMMIFIED BACK THEN?
YES, BUT TERA HAD HER ***OWN*** DOCTORS AND HER ***OWN*** TOMB.
COMBINED WITH INCANTATIONS AND MAGICKS, SHE SAID SHE WOULD ONE DAY RETURN. TERA ALWAYS KEPT HER PROMISES.
WONDERFUL PERFORMANCE FROM AN ACCOMPLISHED CON MAN.
STILL SMUGGLING? OR HAVE YOU MOVED UP INTO THEFT OF PRIVATE PROPERTY?
SERGEANT. JOHN IS A GUEST WITHIN THIS HOUSE.
THAT'S ALRIGHT, MARGARET. SERGEANT DOYLE AND I GO BACK A LONG TIME AND HAVE AN EQUITABLE RELATIONSHIP.
HE HATES ME AND I HAVE OTHER THINGS TO DO RATHER THAN ***THINK*** OF HIM.
LIKE SAVING ABEL'S LIFE.

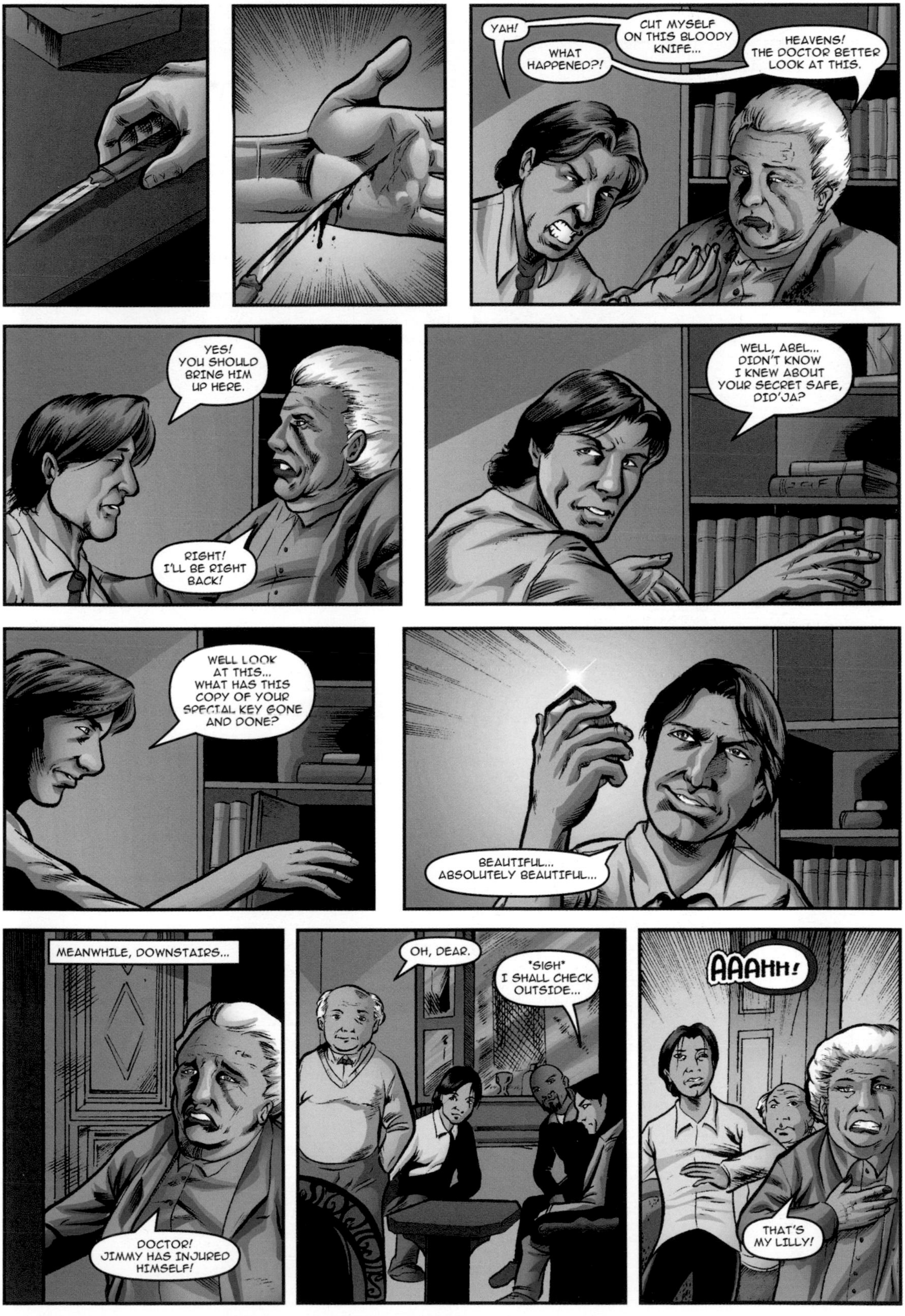
YAH!
WHAT HAPPENED?!
CUT MYSELF ON THIS BLOODY KNIFE...
HEAVENS! THE DOCTOR BETTER LOOK AT THIS.
YES! YOU SHOULD BRING HIM UP HERE.
RIGHT! I'LL BE RIGHT BACK!
WELL, ABEL... DIDN'T KNOW I KNEW ABOUT YOUR SECRET SAFE, DID'JA?
WELL LOOK AT THIS... WHAT HAS THIS COPY OF YOUR SPECIAL KEY GONE AND DONE?
BEAUTIFUL... ABSOLUTELY BEAUTIFUL...
MEANWHILE, DOWNSTAIRS...
DOCTOR! JIMMY HAS INJURED HIMSELF!
OH, DEAR.
SIGH I SHALL CHECK OUTSIDE...
AAAHH!
THAT'S MY LILLY!

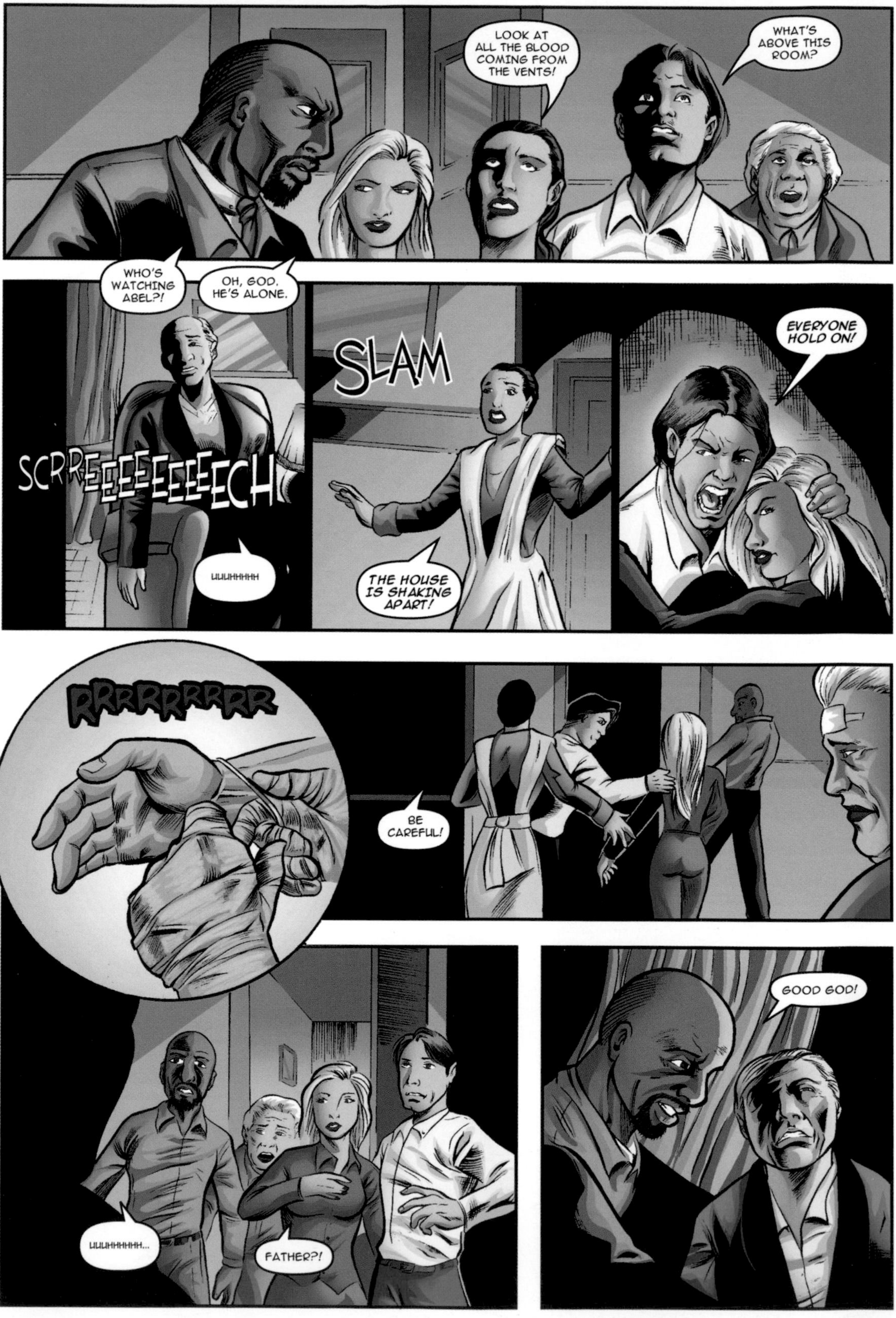
LOOK AT ALL THE BLOOD COMING FROM THE VENTS!
WHAT'S ABOVE THIS ROOM?
WHO'S WATCHING ABEL?!
OH, GOD. HE'S ALONE.
SCRREEEEEEEEEECH
UUUHHHHH
SLAM
THE HOUSE IS SHAKING APART!
EVERYONE HOLD ON!
RRRRRRRRRR
BE CAREFUL!
UUUHHHHHH...
FATHER?!
GOOD GOD!

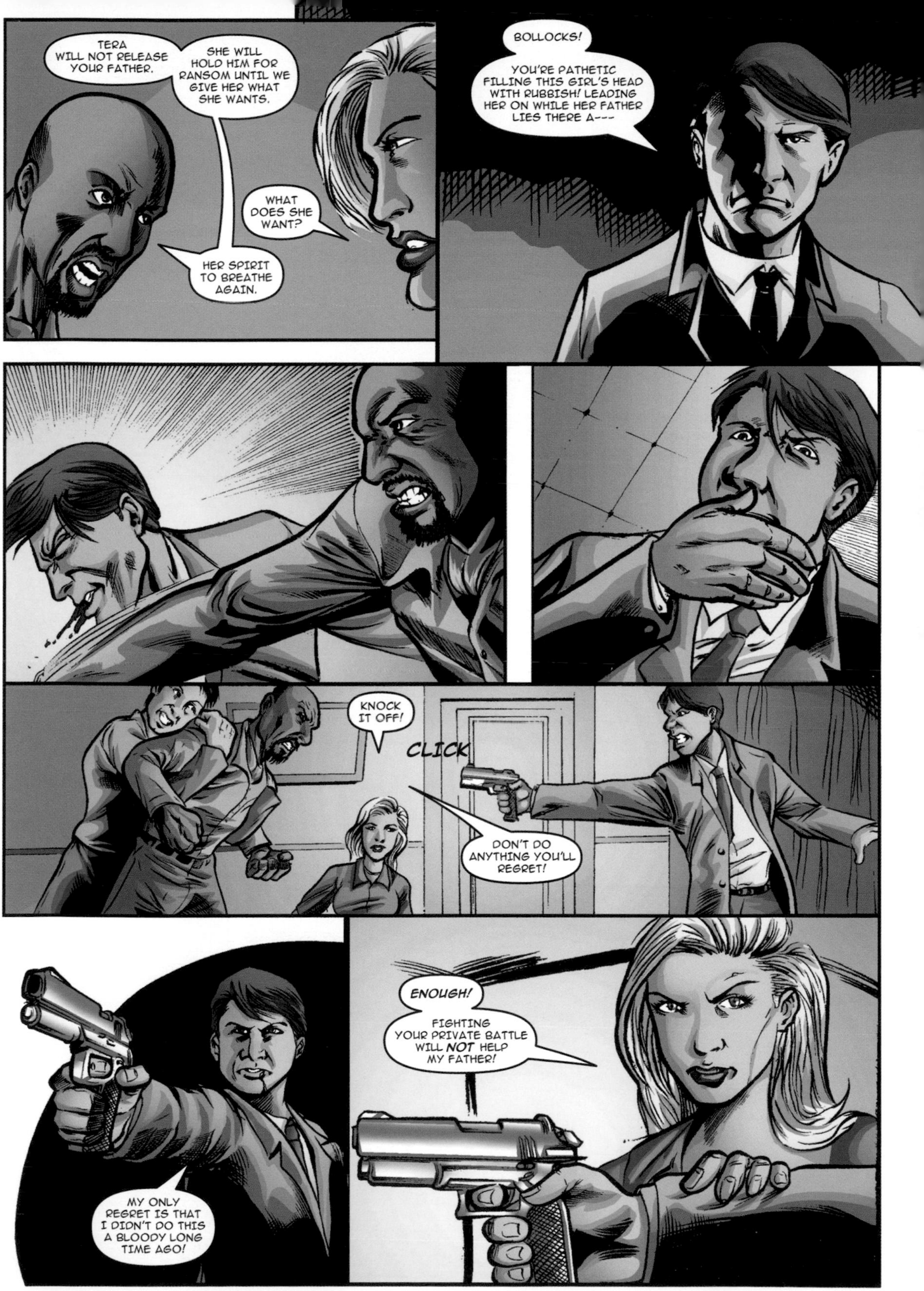
TERA WILL NOT RELEASE YOUR FATHER.
SHE WILL HOLD HIM FOR RANSOM UNTIL WE GIVE HER WHAT SHE WANTS.
WHAT DOES SHE WANT?
HER SPIRIT TO BREATHE AGAIN.
BOLLOCKS!
YOU'RE PATHETIC FILLING THIS GIRL'S HEAD WITH RUBBISH! LEADING HER ON WHILE HER FATHER LIES THERE A---
KNOCK IT OFF!
CLICK
DON'T DO ANYTHING YOU'LL REGRET!
MY ONLY REGRET IS THAT I DIDN'T DO THIS A BLOODY LONG TIME AGO!
ENOUGH!
FIGHTING YOUR PRIVATE BATTLE WILL NOT HELP MY FATHER!

AGGGKKKKK

AKKKK-KKTT

ŭÚśȁ

MARGARET? WHAT ARE YOU DOING?!

śX̌ɔìX̌ɔɓeV́

ɳɕ̇ȁ ȁɕ̇úɔìV̌ȁ

POSSESSED, IS SHE?

WE NEED TO GET HER BACK INSIDE!

WHAT LANGUAGE IS THAT?

ANCIENT EGYPTIAN.

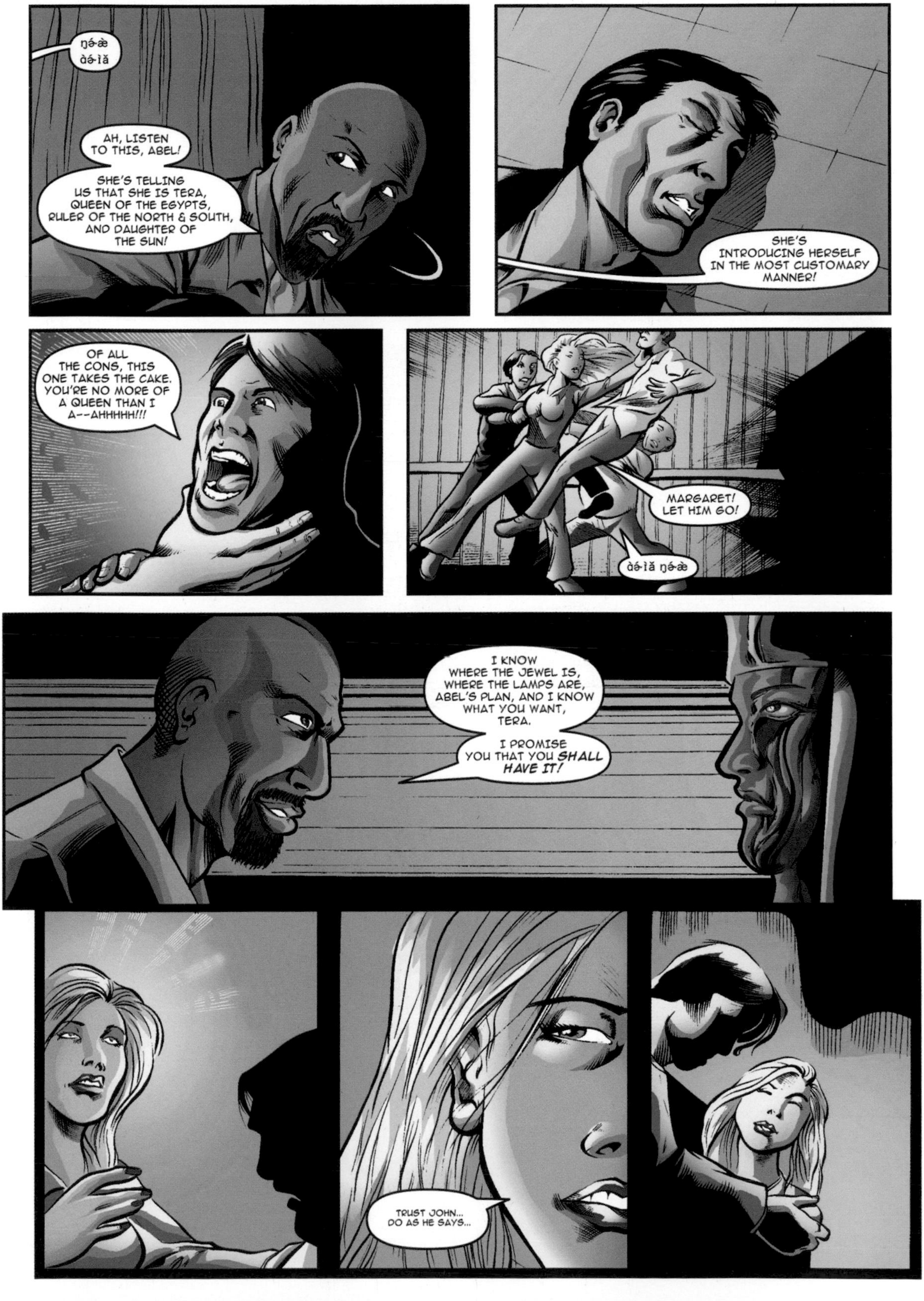
ŋə́-æ̀ ə̀ə́-ĭă
AH, LISTEN TO THIS, ABEL!
SHE'S TELLING US THAT SHE IS TERA, QUEEN OF THE EGYPTS, RULER OF THE NORTH & SOUTH, AND DAUGHTER OF THE SUN!
SHE'S INTRODUCING HERSELF IN THE MOST CUSTOMARY MANNER!
OF ALL THE CONS, THIS ONE TAKES THE CAKE. YOU'RE NO MORE OF A QUEEN THAN I A--AHHHHH!!!
MARGARET! LET HIM GO!
ə̀ə́-ĭă ŋə́-æ̀
I KNOW WHERE THE JEWEL IS, WHERE THE LAMPS ARE, ABEL'S PLAN, AND I KNOW WHAT YOU WANT, TERA.
I PROMISE YOU THAT YOU *SHALL HAVE IT!*
TRUST JOHN... DO AS HE SAYS...

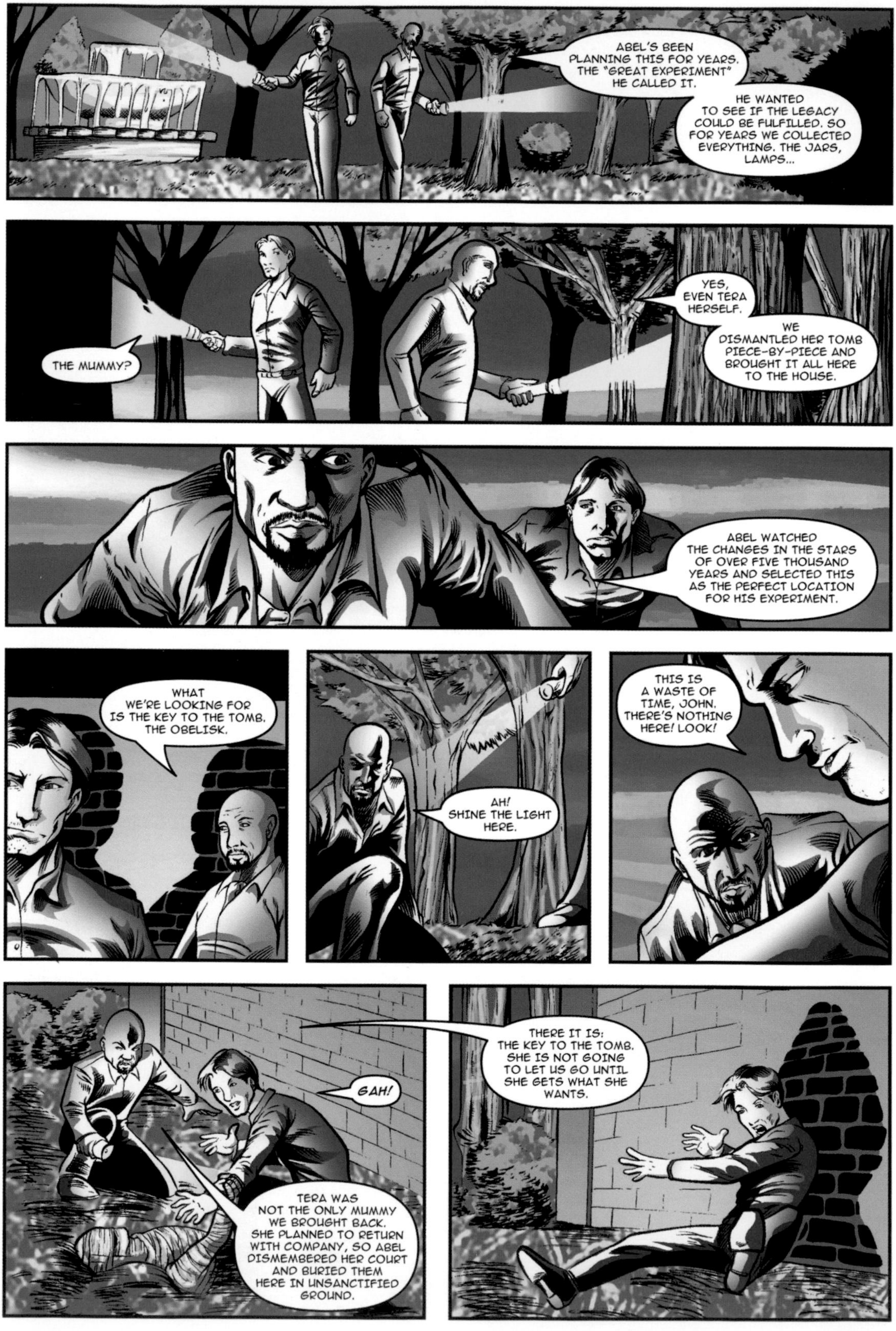
ABEL'S BEEN PLANNING THIS FOR YEARS. THE "GREAT EXPERIMENT" HE CALLED IT.
HE WANTED TO SEE IF THE LEGACY COULD BE FULFILLED. SO FOR YEARS WE COLLECTED EVERYTHING. THE JARS, LAMPS...
THE MUMMY?
YES, EVEN TERA HERSELF.
WE DISMANTLED HER TOMB PIECE-BY-PIECE AND BROUGHT IT ALL HERE TO THE HOUSE.
ABEL WATCHED THE CHANGES IN THE STARS OF OVER FIVE THOUSAND YEARS AND SELECTED THIS AS THE PERFECT LOCATION FOR HIS EXPERIMENT.
WHAT WE'RE LOOKING FOR IS THE KEY TO THE TOMB. THE OBELISK.
AH! SHINE THE LIGHT HERE.
THIS IS A WASTE OF TIME, JOHN. THERE'S NOTHING HERE! LOOK!
GAH!
TERA WAS NOT THE ONLY MUMMY WE BROUGHT BACK. SHE PLANNED TO RETURN WITH COMPANY, SO ABEL DISMEMBERED HER COURT AND BURIED THEM HERE IN UNSANCTIFIED GROUND.
THERE IT IS: THE KEY TO THE TOMB. SHE IS NOT GOING TO LET US GO UNTIL SHE GETS WHAT SHE WANTS.

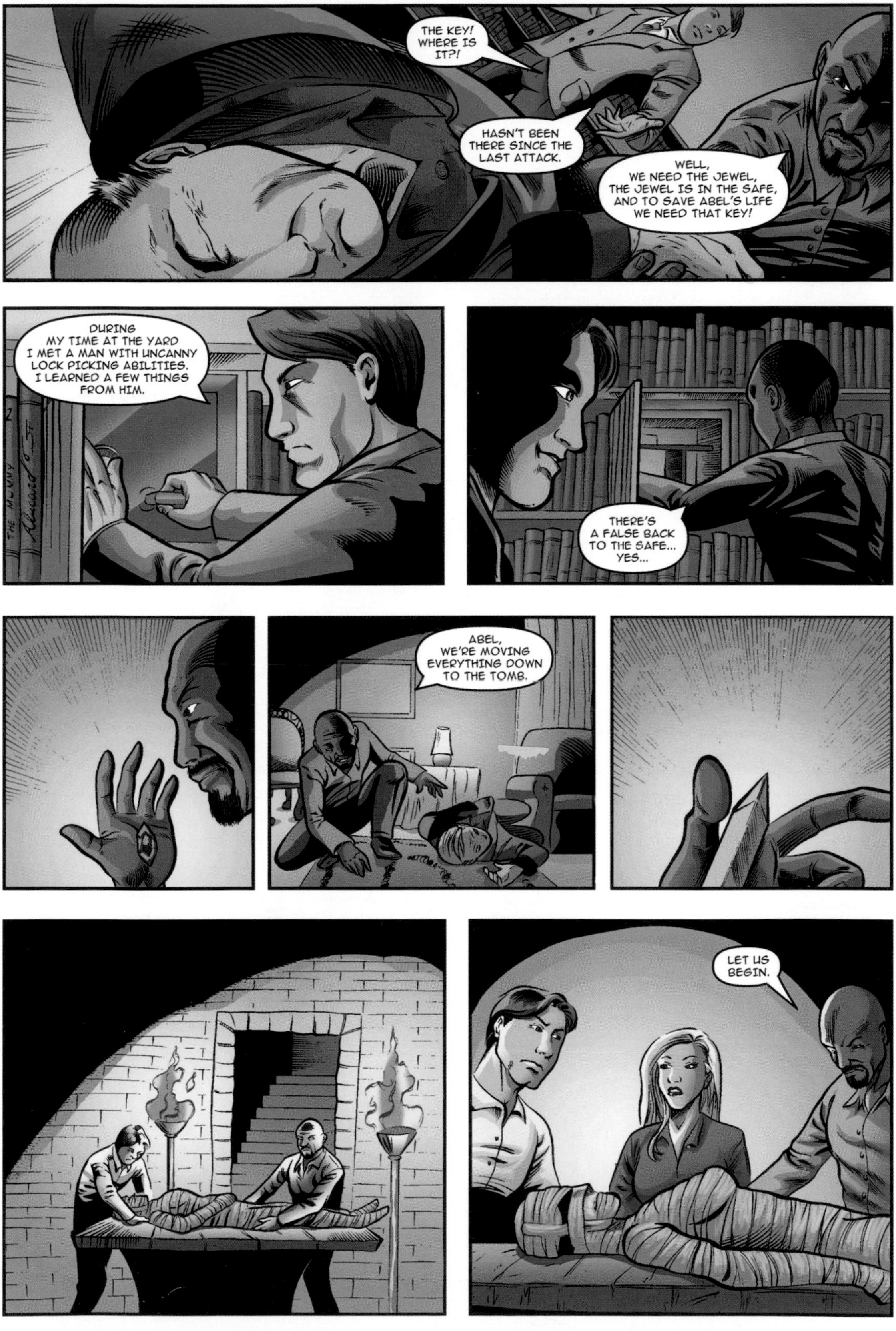
THE KEY! WHERE IS IT?!
HASN'T BEEN THERE SINCE THE LAST ATTACK.
WELL, WE NEED THE JEWEL, THE JEWEL IS IN THE SAFE, AND TO SAVE ABEL'S LIFE WE NEED THAT KEY!
DURING MY TIME AT THE YARD I MET A MAN WITH UNCANNY LOCK PICKING ABILITIES. I LEARNED A FEW THINGS FROM HIM.
THERE'S A FALSE BACK TO THE SAFE... YES...
ABEL, WE'RE MOVING EVERYTHING DOWN TO THE TOMB.
LET US BEGIN.

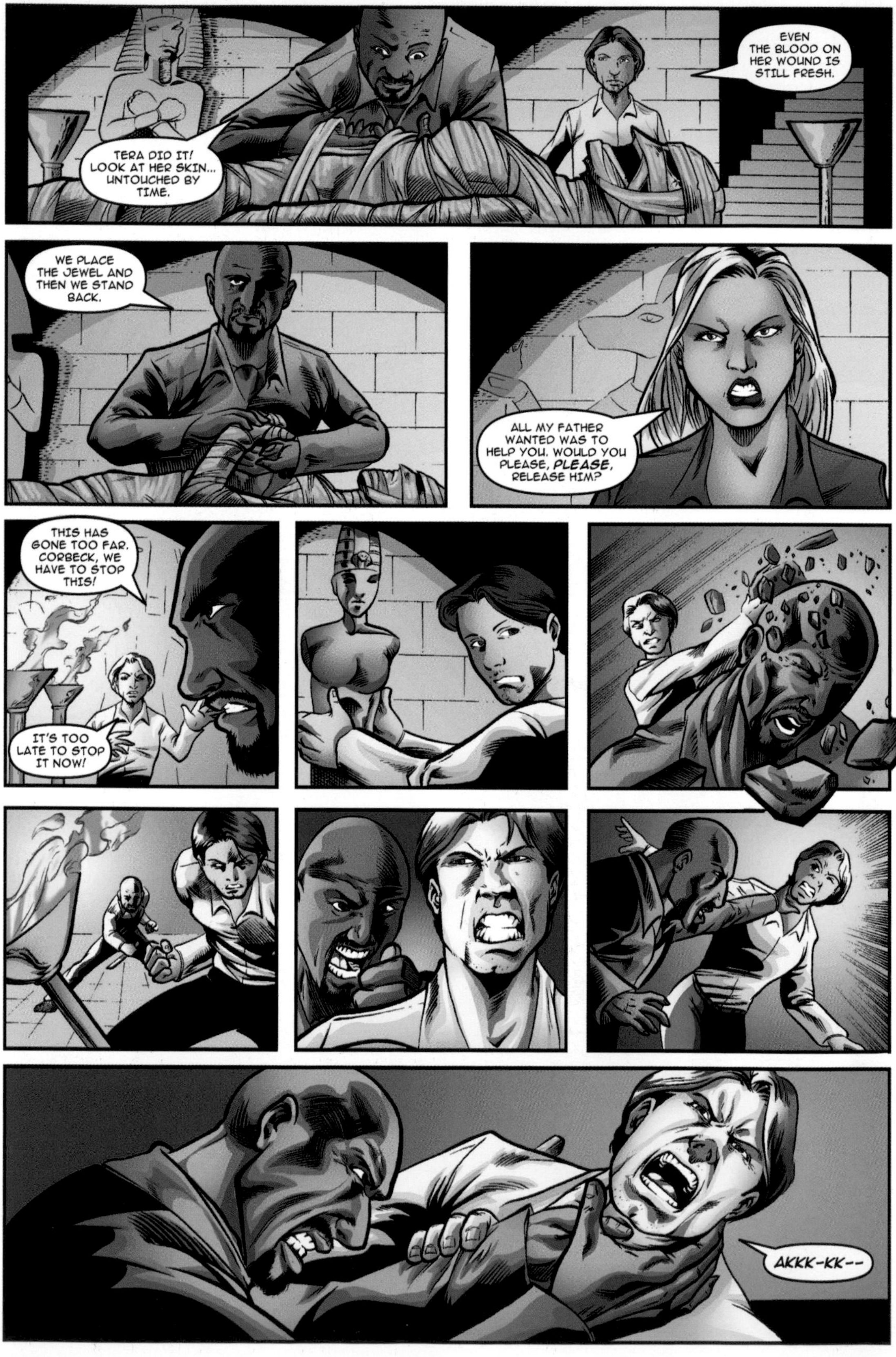

EVEN THE BLOOD ON HER WOUND IS STILL FRESH.
TERA DID IT! LOOK AT HER SKIN... UNTOUCHED BY TIME.
WE PLACE THE JEWEL AND THEN WE STAND BACK.
ALL MY FATHER WANTED WAS TO HELP YOU. WOULD YOU PLEASE, PLEASE, RELEASE HIM?
THIS HAS GONE TOO FAR. CORBECK, WE HAVE TO STOP THIS!
IT'S TOO LATE TO STOP IT NOW!
AKKK-KK--

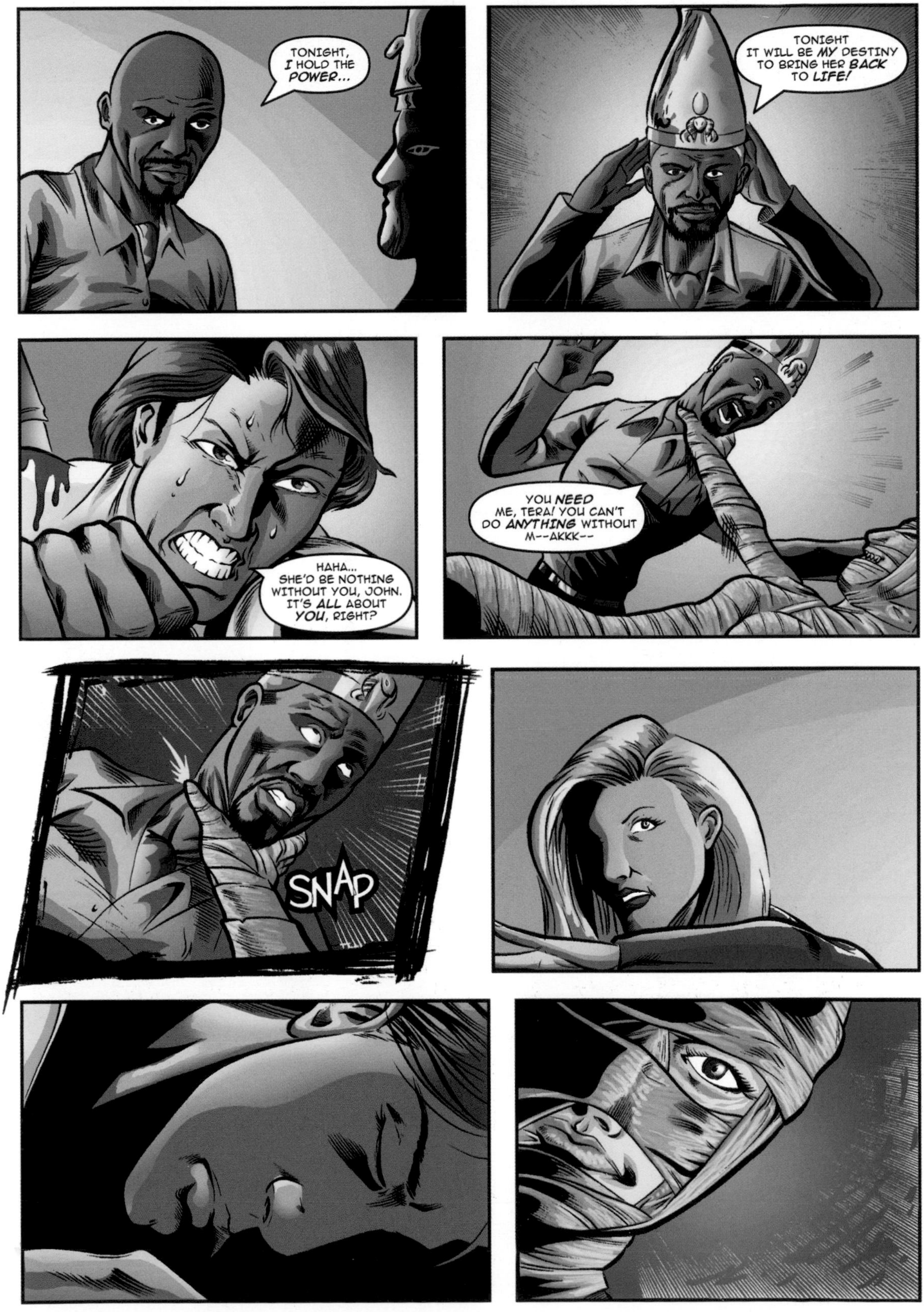

TONIGHT, I HOLD THE POWER...
TONIGHT IT WILL BE MY DESTINY TO BRING HER BACK TO LIFE!
HAHA... SHE'D BE NOTHING WITHOUT YOU, JOHN. IT'S ALL ABOUT YOU, RIGHT?
YOU NEED ME, TERA! YOU CAN'T DO ANYTHING WITHOUT M--AKKK--
SNAP

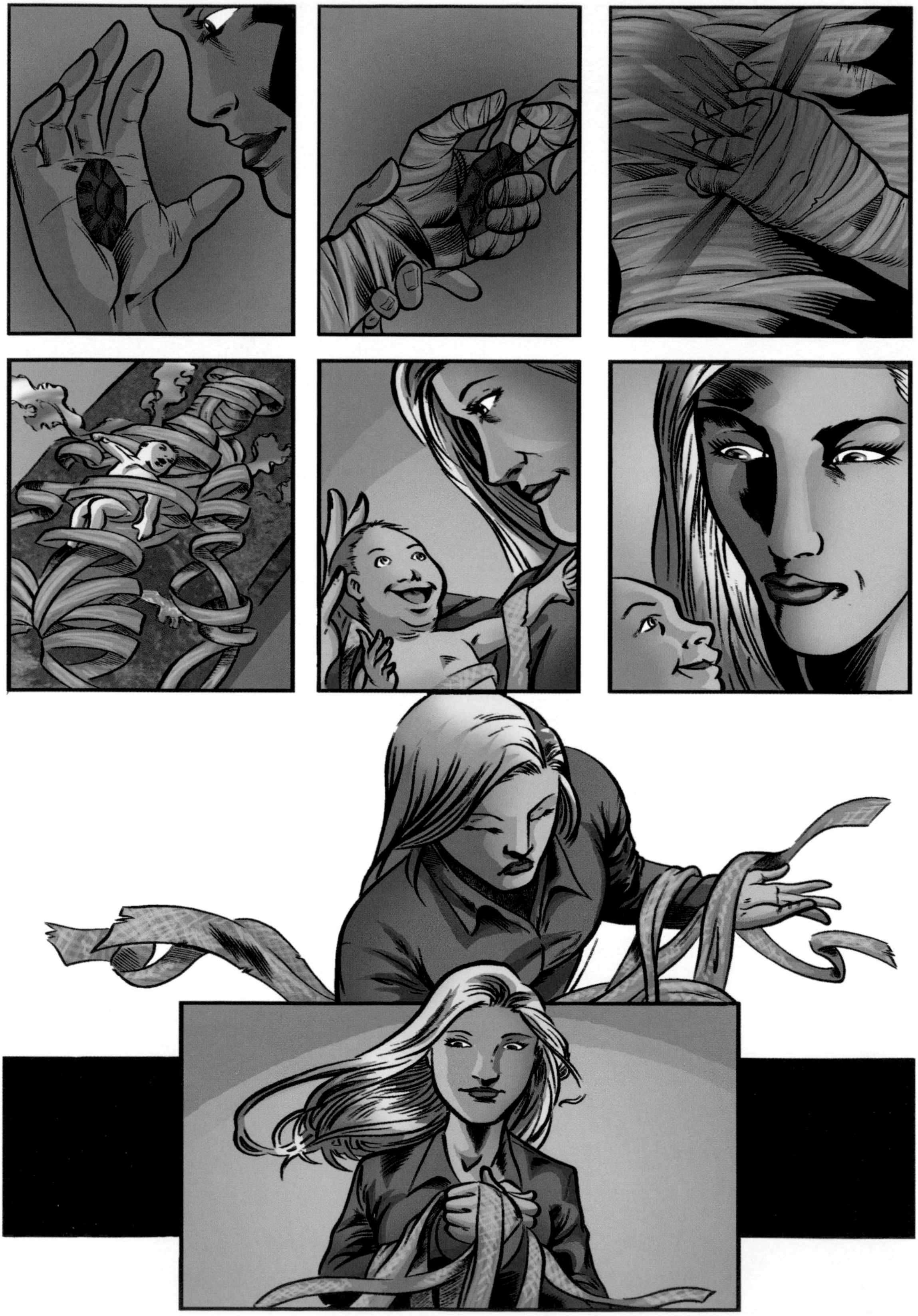

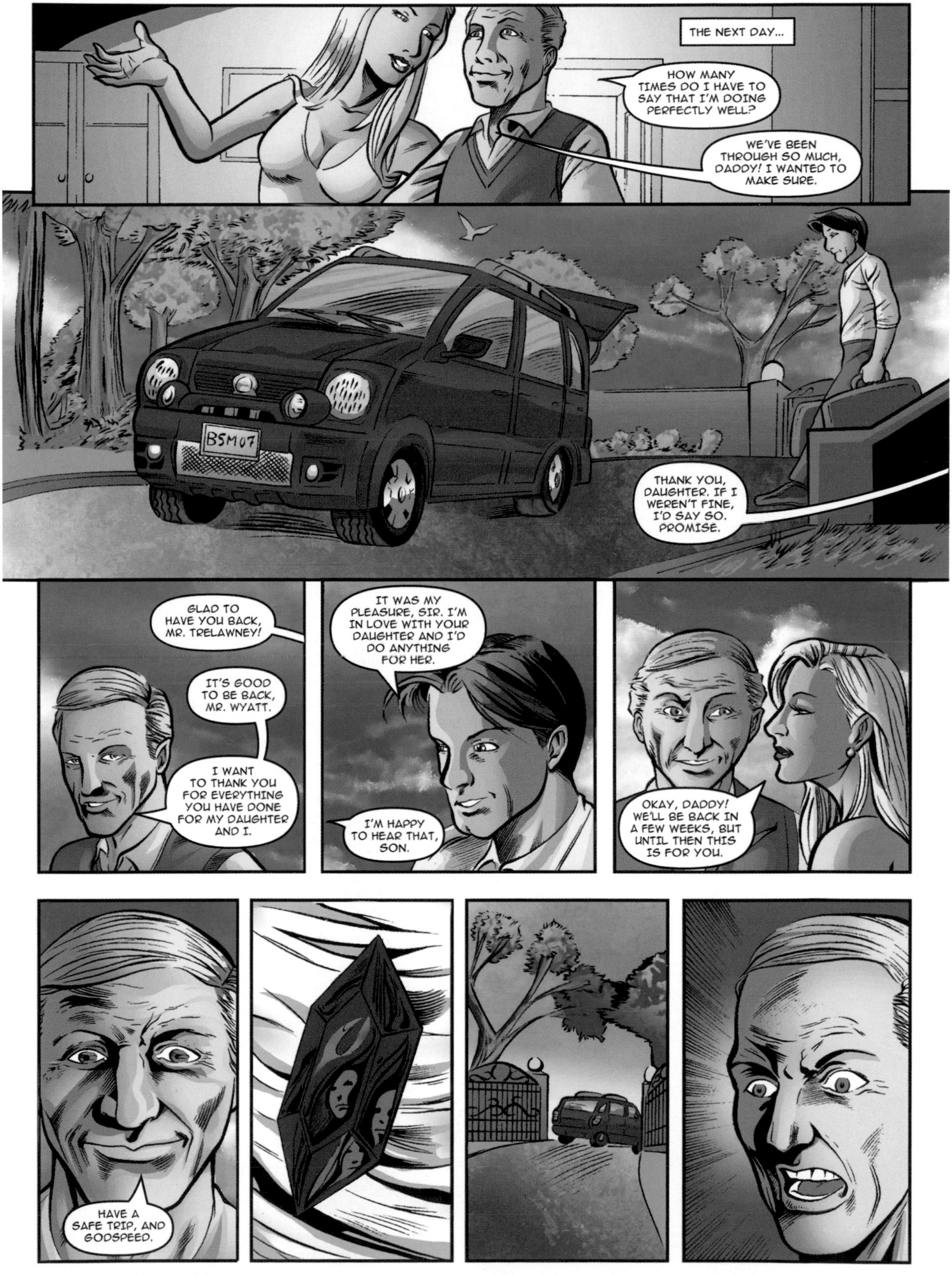
THE NEXT DAY...
HOW MANY TIMES DO I HAVE TO SAY THAT I'M DOING PERFECTLY WELL?
WE'VE BEEN THROUGH SO MUCH, DADDY! I WANTED TO MAKE SURE.
BSM07
THANK YOU, DAUGHTER. IF I WEREN'T FINE, I'D SAY SO. PROMISE.
GLAD TO HAVE YOU BACK, MR. TRELAWNEY!
IT'S GOOD TO BE BACK, MR. WYATT.
I WANT TO THANK YOU FOR EVERYTHING YOU HAVE DONE FOR MY DAUGHTER AND I.
IT WAS MY PLEASURE, SIR. I'M IN LOVE WITH YOUR DAUGHTER AND I'D DO ANYTHING FOR HER.
I'M HAPPY TO HEAR THAT, SON.
OKAY, DADDY! WE'LL BE BACK IN A FEW WEEKS, BUT UNTIL THEN THIS IS FOR YOU.
HAVE A SAFE TRIP, AND GODSPEED.

Bram Stoker

Bram Stoker was born in Dublin, Ireland, on November 8, 1847. He was the third of seven children. Stoker was ill throughout his childhood. Because of this, he did not walk until he was seven years old.

Stoker outgrew his illness and entered the University of Dublin when he was 16. He became an outstanding athlete. While he was at the University, he discovered a passion for theater.

In 1870, Stoker began his work as a civil servant at Dublin Castle. In 1878, he met his idol, actor Sir Henry Irving. He soon accepted a job as Irving's manager. In 1878, he also married Florence Balcombe and moved to London, England.

Stoker's first book was published in 1879. It was a handbook. He later turned to fiction, and his masterpiece, *Dracula*, was published in 1897. Stoker wrote several novels after, but none were as popular as *Dracula*. Bram Stoker died on April 20, 1912, in London. His successful novel has since been enjoyed as plays and films by people around the world.

Stoker Has Many Additional Works Including

The Duties of Clerks of Petty Sessions in Ireland (1879)
The Snake's Pass (1891)
Dracula (1897)
The Mystery of the Sea (1902)
The Jewel of Seven Stars (1904)
The Lady of the Shroud (1909)